IMPERFECT
Match

IMPERFECT
Match

JORDAN CASTILLO PRICE

jcpbooks.com

Print edition published in the
United States in 2018 by JCP Books
www.jcpbooks.com

First Print Edition

ISBN 978-1-935540-99-1

Audio edition available

1

WEDDINGS WERE SUPPOSED TO be happy occasions. Right?

Lee cast his gaze across the empty hall and wished he could dredge up some semblance of enthusiasm for the speech he'd be expected to deliver tomorrow. According to his research—and Lee *adored* research—the twenty-third century had been rife with pithy, quotable sayings. Funny, he hadn't found anything pithy. Or quotable. Or even remotely encouraging. Just a bunch of blathering about fertility and duty.

Something contemporary, then. "Happiness and Hope, and welcome...welcome? Thank you for coming?" He wrote *Happiness and Hope* in his notebook, crossed it out, then wrote it again. "Happiness and Hope, and welcome to this, uh...heartwarming celebration where my cherished sister, Emma, has been united in wedded bliss to her perfect match, Harold."

"Howard."

"Damn it." Lee squinted toward the back of the hall to see who'd corrected him. A menacing figure was backlit in the doorway. Well, maybe not menacing, but at least unexpected. At this hour, he'd figured the place would be empty. It *should* have been empty. "How about a little privacy here?"

"There's nearly three hundred people on the guest list, and you're worrying if one wedding lackey overhears you practicing your speech?"

Yes. Because there was no speech. Two years in the planning, and there was no speech. "Listen, whoever you are—"

"Roman Sharp. Caterer by day, waiter by night. I know, I know, hoarding all the glamor jobs for myself. Just call me insatiable."

"Isn't there anywhere else you can work? I'm running out of time to get my speech together."

"And I need to make sure this place is ready for the big day." Roman stepped into the light. Not exactly menacing. Well, maybe a bit. The sort of guy whose appearance would remind you to lock your car, anyhow. He sauntered down the center of the banquet hall, hands in pockets, his stiff black-on-black caterer's uniform angling harshly over elbow, shoulder and knee. His hair was black too, poker-straight, side-parted and falling across one eye. If Lee's hair ever did that, he would've been raking it off his face by now. He'd never been much good at playing it cool. The caterer stopped in front of the bride's table, planted his hands on his hips, looked him up and down, and said, "Look, I've catered two dozen Boomer weddings in the last month alone, so speeches? I've heard 'em all."

If Roman's lyrical drawl hadn't been a dead giveaway as to where he lived, his use of the term *Boomer* certainly would have. Vernacular revealed so much about the speaker.

"Well, go on," Roman said. "You couldn't ask for a better audience."

Probably not. If Lee couldn't handle one person

staring at him, three hundred would be absolutely paralyzing. He cleared his throat, squared his shoulders, checked his notes, and began. "Happiness and Hope, and—"

"Isn't it weird how people greet each other with 'Happiness and Hope' nowadays? They didn't used to."

"It's been a pretty standard North American greeting since the rebuilding years, especially east of Mississippi and throughout Canada."

"Is that so?" Roman's eyebrows twitched in amusement. "Eating dictionaries for breakfast never smoothed out any toasts that I know of."

Lee considered informing the worker that extensive etymology wasn't typical of the average dictionary, but he suspected it would only earn him an eye-roll. "I'm a language major...and Happiness and Hope seems like the appropriate thing to say. It is a wedding, after all."

"As if every single day is brimming with optimism and delight. Remember when it wasn't rude to say 'how are you?' Like when we were kids?"

"Maybe where you grew up." The Taxable District, clearly. "I've only heard 'how are you?' in old movies."

"Lately people act like you're calling them a plague-carrier if you imply they're anything less than fantastic."

Lee might as well be a plague-carrier if he couldn't pull it together by the time the reception started. "Look, it's my sister's wedding and I'm starting with 'Happiness and Hope.' Anything else would be upsetting."

Roman cocked a hip, crossed his arms, and gave a smirk that suggested *upsetting* was entirely preferable to the pedestrian words coming out of Lee's mouth.

Lee ignored him. "Happiness and Hope, and welcome to the celebration of...uh...."

"Of your sister getting hitched to this Howard guy."

"Of the day when my sister embarks on the next stage of her life with...her love? Her loving, um...."

"Some guy the Algorithm matched her with when your mother chose to keep the pregnancy?"

Lee crouched low on the stage and hissed, "What is your problem? Someone might have heard!"

"Someone did hear. You."

"I need to lie down." Head swimming, Lee stumbled off the shallow stage, past the mounds of coiled streamers, folded tablecloths and uninflated balloons. A broad bench spanned the far side of the banquet hall, a lightly padded stretch where people would perch while they nibbled canapés and endured the stilted wedding music. He collapsed onto the cushions and draped an arm across his eyes, though he left a small gap so he could track the caterer's approach.

Roman strolled over and planted himself directly beside Lee's head with a graceless thunk. "Not that I think you're a plague-carrier...but are you okay?"

Where the hell had this guy learned his manners, out back behind the dumpsters? 'Are you okay?' was even worse than 'how are you?'

Lee moaned. "Is this some kind of tradition—hazing the wedding party? Did Harold put you up to this?"

"You mean Howard?" Roman teased. "Nope. Never met the guy. Have you? 'Cos it doesn't seem like he's made much of an impression."

"What am I going to do? My mom will harp on me for the rest of my life if I call him *Harold* when I give the toast."

"Jot down his name."

"I'm not going to read from my notes. They're just for practice."

"Then write it on your palm."

"Oh, that's pretty smooth." Plus, he'd likely sweat it right back off.

"Or think up a hint to jog your memory. Like, *How weird is Howard?*"

"You're not making this any easier."

"Set it to music and you're good to go. I'd sing it to you, but that wouldn't be much help. You'd need a familiar tune, and I doubt we have the same taste in bands."

Lee expected him to belt out something just the same. When he didn't, Lee pried open one squinting eye and said, "What's that supposed to mean?"

"Just that I've never seen you down by the Bonfires. I would've remembered."

"You've actually been...there?"

"Whenever I'm not working, that's where you'll find me. Tonight, for instance—your rehearsal dinner's not on my schedule." No. Apparently, Howard's father was trying to prove something by holding it at his country club—at least according to Mom, that was why. "You should come. Check out the band. Get a few free drinks in you beforehand, meet me out back...."

Images of the Bonfires blazed in Lee's imagination, the jerky footage he'd seen on the news of a rage-filled hardcore band, churning crowds, and massive fires shooting sparks up into the night sky. He wouldn't have pictured himself at the Bonfires any more than he might have seen himself robbing a bank, or asking his sister if Howard was anywhere near as creepy as he seemed. "Right. Me. At the Bonfires."

"Why not? It's easy enough to find. Head toward the river, listen for the music, and keep an eye peeled for the ginormous glowing fiery-looking things."

Getting there wasn't the problem. *Being* there was,

especially after dark. "People get killed," Lee murmured.

"That hardly ever happens." Roman smoothed Lee's hair off his forehead, just the casual brush of fingertips, and at the feel of the casually inappropriate touch, Lee's eyes shot open wide. "And usually it's the ones itching for a fight who end up getting exactly what they came for. I'm no fighter. Sure, I can handle myself, but that's not why I go."

Lee suddenly felt entirely too vulnerable, lying there supine with a stranger close enough to touch. He scrambled into a sitting position and said, "Why *do* you go?"

Roman held Lee's gaze for an overlong and scurrilously direct moment, then wet his lips and slowly smiled. "For the music. Why else?"

Lee wasn't sure. But his pulse was pounding so hard he could hear it in his eardrums, like echoes of the newscasts where the reporters shook their heads and spoke in muted, sympathetic tones while behind them, mayhem raged in the Tax District. He imagined one of the Bonfire bands setting up on the banquet hall's shallow stage, all tattoos and piercings and matted, filthy hair, tearing through a set while the guests backed against the far wall in horror, upsetting the wishing well and flattening the wedding cake. Now *that* would be a wedding to remember.

"What kind of band played at your wedding?" Lee asked the caterer.

"Who says I'm married?"

"You're not? Oh. I just figured...."

Roman sat there smirking at him until Lee dropped his gaze. "Yeah, I know," Roman said, "I'm getting kinda ripe. But do you know the going rate for a wedding tax?"

"Not really." Lee's father was the one who handled

the household budget.

"Five hundred percent. So if the rental hall costs a grand, another five grand goes to some bloated bureaucrat's coffers."

"That can't be right. The Tax Moderation Act caps off taxation at 99%."

"In theory. But think about it. There's federal tax. Then add state, county, city and district. Weddings fall under all five jurisdictions. Like passports. Litigations. Funerals. Everyone on your side of the tracks—people with benefits—ties the knot before they're thirty...not that they have much say in the matter. But it's not mandatory where I live, and it costs so much, lots of us don't bother."

"I'm sorry."

"For what?"

Lee wasn't really sure.

"If it wasn't for all you Benefit Boomers racing toward the altar, I'd be stuck catering business networking socials. And if you think weddings are dull...." They sat in a silence that was more awkward than companionable, until Roman asked, "So...who played your wedding?"

The question was innocent enough. Logical, too, given that Roman was in the wedding business. There was no way he could've known that Lee was filled with such dread over the thought of meeting his preordained bride, he'd switched his major five times to keep himself buffered by an ever-shifting course load and a degree that was always safely out of reach. "I'm not married," Lee admitted.

"I know."

"How?"

Roman stood and crossed to the bar, which was

covered with a drop cloth. He lifted a corner of the fabric and began rummaging in the cabinet. "I'm good at reading body language."

"I have *single* body language?"

"Maybe you do." Roman pulled out a bottle of clear liquor and held it up to the light. "Or maybe a look at the seating chart told me you don't have a wife next to you. In any case, this calls for a toast."

"It's not even noon."

"It's noon somewhere." Roman cracked open the top and took a long pull straight from the bottle. "To bachelorhood." He tipped the neck toward Lee in invitation, but Lee knew if he started drinking now, he'd be plastered by the time the rehearsal started.

"No. I'd better not." But he wanted to. He stepped back onstage and looked out over the empty hall, and told himself that he just needed to assemble a few sentences on love and happiness and new beginnings, and then he could drink enough cocktails to ensure he got some sleep before his sister's big day. Or meet up with Roman and go to the Bonfires. Which, obviously, he was too big of a wimp to actually do. "You hear these speeches all the time, don't you? What the heck do people say?"

Roman planted himself in a chair at the bride's table, tipped back in his seat so it teetered on its hind legs, cradled the bottle against his midriff, and thought. "Let's see. Thank everyone for coming. Cheesy joke—optional, but more common than you'd think. Heartwarming anecdote about the friend or family member who's getting their big sendoff. Observation about how suitably the Algorithm matched the new bride and groom. Eagerness to see what kind of sturdy offspring they'll have. Then an invitation to start drinking." He took another slug from the bottle—straight vodka? Lee shuddered. "It's all filler, when you come right down to it. People wanna get a look at the spouse so they can gossip later, and they wanna get plowed. Get your new brother-in-law's name right and you can say just about anything. By the end of the night, no one will even remember."

Go with the flow. Right. Lee was good at that.

Roman took another long drink. A big bubble glugged to the top, and he lowered it with a brisk, "Ahh!"

"Is that watered down?"

"Nope." Roman held out the bottle again and shook it playfully. "You sure I can't tempt you?"

"Warm? Straight up? No. Thanks."

"So you're saying the fact that it's still technically morning is no longer a factor. Because I know where the ice would be, and I'm sure I could find a mixer—vodka's versatile that way." Before Lee could figure out how to backpedal, Roman grabbed him by the wrist, tugged him off the shallow stage, and dragged him through the kitchen doors.

2

THE KITCHEN WAS DARK—COOL and still. It smelled like bleach with a distant undertone of grease. The stainless steel tabletops gleamed dully in the ambient light of the emergency exit. Roman dragged Lee through to a walk-in cooler, flicked on a light and surveyed the shelves. Most of the stuff was in plain white boxes, nothing like commercial food with its logos and slogans. "Huh," Roman said. "Things are a little more scarce here than I would've hoped. Maybe there's some Bloody Mary mix out by the bar. No celery, but hey, beggars can't be choosers. And as for ice...." He shuffled boxes, pawed through all the shelves, then set his sights on a tall shape in back, swaddled in a plastic tarp. "Hey, now."

Lee didn't realize what Roman was unveiling until light from the bare bulb overhead glinted off its surface. "Wait! Don't touch that."

"I thought you needed ice."

Roman tossed aside the tarp and presented the sculpture with a flourish. Flowers. Massive flowers. Some clear, some frosted white. No doubt there was discussion over the detailing. After hearing about calla lilies versus roses for the duration of an excruciating dinner, Lee had tuned the discussion out.

"My family fought about that stupid sculpture for nearly a week."

"Is that so?" Roman pulled a jackknife from his pocket and gave the back of the statue an unceremonious jab. Lee stared in horror. A few more quick stabs, and the tip of a petal came loose. Roman flicked the ice fragment toward Lee. "Heads up!"

Lee caught it, pure reflex. Only then did he realize it was so cold it burned, and started shifting it hand to hand. Roman licked his thumb and smoothed over the spot where he'd hacked off a piece. "Guess we should've found a cup first. I might be a tad buzzed. C'mon."

While Roman strode from the walk-in cooler, Lee lingered. He glanced quickly at the back of the ice sculpture, sure there'd be a gigantic wound where Roman had mutilated the artistry, but try as he might, he couldn't quite see where the deed had been done. Just hills and valleys of ice. He took one final look at the front, with its glassy stylized plaque engraved with a pair of wedding rings, and below that, the words, *Happiness, Hope and Love - Emma and Howard*.

Love. Right. Emma hardly even knew the guy. He whisked the tarp over it hastily, one-handed, and followed Roman into the kitchen. It was indeed noon somewhere. And maybe a drink would calm him down enough to come up with the forgettable toast he was responsible for making.

"Here you go." Roman shoved a measuring cup into Lee's hands and dumped in a good slosh of vodka. He might have worked countless weddings, but clearly not behind the bar, given the generosity of his serving. He hauled open the door of an industrial fridge.

"Bingo. Lemon juice. A dash of that, a packet of sugar, and you've got yourself a vodka sour. Not a particularly good vodka sour, at least by Boomer standards. But a drink's a drink."

Lee dropped in his ice hunk. "What do you mean, Boomer standards?"

"Booze falls into the 500% markup bracket. It's all bathtub gin where I live. So, this?" Roman hoisted the bottle and took a long, deep drink. "This sparkles across my palate like the newly driven snow, glittering in the sunrise of a crisp December morning."

While Roman tipped back another swallow, Lee felt a pang. Not just apprehension or worry, but guilt. He took a tentative sip from his measuring cup and wondered if he tasted winter too, or if he only wished he could.

Roman didn't notice Lee's introspective mood shift— or maybe he just thought he was still fretting about his speech. Which he was. But not nearly as urgently as before. "So what about the wedding itself?" Roman asked. "I've got the details in writing, right down to which way the centerpieces are supposed to face. But the big question is: to clink, or not to clink."

"Clink what?"

"Spoons on glasses."

"People don't really do that."

Roman smirked. "They must. Otherwise you wouldn't know what I meant."

How *did* Lee know? He'd never been in a wedding crowd gauche enough to expect the newlyweds to kiss at the reception, right there in front of every-one—especially not on command. Must've been the remnants of an old, forgotten movie...or a horror story passed around the campfire. "We'd never do that to

Emma. Bad enough it'll happen at the altar."

"Oh, come on, don't be a stick in the mud." Roman grabbed a serving spoon off a hook and started rapping it on the stainless steel table. "Kiss...kiss...kiss...."

"Tell me that doesn't happen at your District weddings."

"Not only does it happen—it's the highlight of the evening."

Lee felt himself blushing from the pit of his belly to the tips of his ears. And he'd only had a single sip of vodka. "Some stranger's mouth mashing against yours. Their spit. Their tongue. Their breath." He shuddered vigorously. "Can you imagine?"

Roman dropped the spoon and gazed down into the vodka bottle with an enigmatic half-smile. "I can." He glanced up coyly and said, "You want to ask me about it? Go ahead. I don't mind. Maybe it'll even take some of the sting off seeing some Howard guy's lips coming at your kid sister."

Lee gawked.

"Oh, come on," Roman said. "You're no virgin. I know for a fact that sex ed is mandatory in your schools."

"It's not required in the District?"

"Heck, no. It's an elective. I took advanced business math instead. Why bother paying for something you can get for free?"

Where? Lee almost blurted out the question, but before he made even more of an idiot out of himself, throngs of people roiling around the Bonfires sprang to mind. Maybe not everybody was dancing or fighting. And they might not even be married. The sudden urge to see the Taxable District by the red, flickering light was strong, though of course Lee would never dream of venturing across Main Street after dark, even with an escort. He was too soft. Too middle-class. He'd probably find himself face-down in the gutter with his wallet and his shoes missing before the first band even finished their set.

His eyes met Roman's. The caterer wasn't really smiling anymore. And he was watching Lee with a disturbing intensity. "Teacher showed you how to assume the position," Roman said, "and how to keep your little swimmers healthy by clearing out the pipes—but she never kissed you."

"No." Lee's mouth formed the word, though nothing managed to come out. After a few deep breaths, he found his voice and said, "So that's not how it is, in the District?"

"Sex ed? Only for the families who think that if they scrimp and save, if they submit the right application and bribe the right bureaucrat, they'll shoehorn their way into the Benefit Sector. They make their kids take all those useless Boomer courses, hoping they'll eventually fit in. The rest of us know better than to bother trying. Especially people like me who work outside the District. I see how things really are around here. Cheaper? Safer? Cleaner? No doubt. But the payoff? Everybody's miserable."

Funny. Lee had never thought of himself as miserable. Why did the word feel so apt?

"I imagine kissing someone wouldn't be nearly as much fun if you didn't have any choice in the matter," Roman said.

Lee had always done his best not to imagine kissing anyone at all. Aside from all the microbes and contaminants—which, admittedly, he knew from his three years of Plague Theory were basically harmless on the average North American mouth—there was the sheer intimacy of the act to contend with. In front of dozens, maybe hundreds, of your family's most important acquaintances. Which Emma would soon be doing. In this very hall. Before the weekend was over.

"Last night," Lee whispered, "I heard my sister crying. Right through the wall. Muffled, like maybe she was face-down on her pillow. But it was late, everything else was totally quiet. And I heard."

"I'm sorry."

"For what?" Lee asked. "You didn't write the Algorithm."

Roman rounded the table, took the measuring cup from Lee's hand, gave the contents a sniff, then handed it back to Lee. "Look, it's not the end of the world. She'll adapt."

"But that's not how things should be. This is supposed to be about happiness. For real. Not just some empty fucking greeting."

Roman raised his eyebrows high. "The swearing sounds especially filthy when one of you Boomers finally lets loose."

"Fuck you." Lee tilted back his measuring cup and tossed back the vodka in one long, satisfying gulp.

"Now you're just showing off."

Lee reached for the vodka. Roman didn't resist, exactly, but he didn't release it either. Instead, he let Lee pull him close along with the bottle, until they were right up against each other. The only liberty he took was to tip in an extra few ounces when Lee poured another drink. "Seriously, though," Roman said. "All the Boomer etiquette of who gets to do what in bed, and when, to whom, how long, and even what position... it's only a matter of time before your population goes into a total tailspin." Instead of drawing back once he'd had his say, Roman lingered there, startlingly close, and gazed deep into Lee's eyes. "Maybe married life will suit your sister." Roman leaned in even closer. Or maybe it was Lee. "I've heard all about your sex ed, and trust me. It's nothing like the real deal."

Whoever it was that closed the gap between them, Lee didn't know. Maybe they were both to blame. Thighs touched. Then chests. Then lips. Roman's mouth blazed with heat, but it tasted like winter. Or maybe just vodka, but Lee was too stunned to dwell on such mundane details. The thought that he had no idea what he was doing, none whatsoever, was blaring through his mind like a pathogen alert. Lee did not simply *do* something. He read about the topic first, streamed some instructional video. He quizzed his professors about the subject and engaged in some mental rehearsal.

But there was no preparing for this first kiss—especially given how scrupulously Lee had avoided the altar.

The sensation was nothing like he'd expected. It tingled, and not just the vodka. The wetness that Lee thought he'd find revolting was intriguingly slick. And the gust of vaporous, compound-laden breath he'd been braced against was only a tantalizing whisper.

Lee didn't return the breath. Not because the thought of exhaling against someone's lips terrified him—though it did—but because he'd forgotten how to work his own lungs. He had no idea what to do with his mouth either, or his face, or his entire body, and yet it seemed that Roman was able to coax his lips apart. The touch of Roman's tongue was such a shock, Lee's breathing ability returned in a great gasp, embarrassingly loud, so mortifying he had to turn away and knuckle the wetness from his lips in shame.

Roman eased back, looking nearly as stunned as Lee

felt, eyes wide, lips parted. His open expression was at odds with the angularity of his body, which looked like it had been built only for decisiveness and action, not the contemplation of the deeper meaning of sex, and kissing, and life. "I'd appreciate it if you didn't mention this to your parents."

"No. Of course I—no."

"I can't get fired. Two-day job, weekend rate, over-time—I need this gig. Rent's coming due."

"I'd never do that."

Even if Lee did say something, who would believe him?

3

INITIALLY, LEE WAS CONCERNED that someone might notice his silence at the rehearsal dinner at a time when he was expected to be intelligent, friendly and charming—though not too intelligent, in case his future in-laws would find him arrogant. Not so friendly as to appear crass. And certainly not charming enough to seem glib. But Howard's father dominated the conversation to the point where Lee couldn't have gotten a word in if he tried.

It was probably a blessing, since Lee felt neither intelligent, nor friendly, nor charming. Mostly, he felt confused.

When the tuxedoed waiters streamed from the kitchen, Lee's confusion intensified. Because obviously Roman was still back in the banquet hall setting up for tomorrow's festivities. But as the waitstaff trooped out to the table with every course, one dedicated waiter per person, Lee couldn't help but scrutinize each one to ensure he wasn't the man whose mouth tasted like winter.

But, no. They wouldn't be. Not only because Roman was still arranging place settings and curling streamers in the banquet hall, but because none of the waiters were District boys like Roman. They were more like Lee, college kids who worked a few hours a week, Boomers with straight white teeth and pale, elegantly tapered fingers. Probably. The supposition that they lacked calluses and hangnails was pure speculation on Lee's part, since their hands were all covered by spotless gloves, but he knew enough Boomers to field an educated guess.

Lee's waiter was nothing like Roman. He might even be the antithesis of Roman. Butter-colored hair, eyes as blue-gray as the veining of a fine Roquefort, skin like homogenized milk. The poor waiter looked so manicured and pampered, if he encountered Roman in a dark alleyway, he'd probably curdle.

He placed a covered dish in front of Lee, and with half an eye on the waiter beside him, lifted the dome, in tandem, with a quiet flourish.

Splayed on a ruffled green bed was a minuscule chicken—plucked naked, legs spread, cavity gaping.

"Wild squab," Howard's father announced with a satisfaction that hinted it was the priciest thing on the menu. "Nothing's too good for the newest member of our family."

Lee couldn't say whether Emma had any reaction to the bragging. He couldn't see her from the far end of the table where he was seated across from his future sister-in-law, a bored teenager in braces. He took a furtive glance at the teenager to see what she made of the squab, but she'd taken no notice of the provocative bird. Her gaze was fixed on the fiber-optic centerpiece that was undulating with subtle shades of turquoise and coral—which were most definitely not the wedding colors.

Across the table and two seats down from Lee, his mother caught his eye and indicated with a meaningful glance the way she held her fork. Lee dutifully located the corresponding fork in his overcrowded place setting and hefted it, all the while wondering if anyone else found their entree disturbingly obscene. How could they not? They'd all been through sex ed, even the girl in braces. Some of them were even married, so they potentially had intercourse just for the fun of it...as difficult as that might be to imagine. Maybe they were so busy figuring out which fork to use that they didn't notice the nudity of the taut, golden skin, or the suggestive cant of the squab's bent knees.

Or maybe it was just that they didn't have the ghost of a recent kiss lingering on their lips.

Silver rang on fine china as the dinner guests began dismantling their birds. Lee had difficulty choosing an entry point. The thigh joint seemed like an obvious place, but as he set his knife against it, eleventh-grade images of Ms. Carmichael flooded his mind—waxed, spread, gleaming with lubricant, benignly helpful and vaguely preoccupied. He'd dutifully slid his hands down her torso, pausing when his thumbs met the crook of her thighs, startled by the hardness of the ligament that ran from groin to hip like a length of industrial cable. If Lee had been with a lover, he would have paused to trace the line of it and see where it led, how it was connected, and whether it tickled when he grazed it with his fingertips. But school was school. Ms. Carmichael had instructed him to spread her labia, and so he did.

The squab's legs gaped.

Lee wondered how egregious the breach of etiquette would be to rotate his plate so the bird's breast faced him instead. He settled for nudging the cavity to five o'clock, and poked the skin a few more times. The teenager across from him tore open a thigh and emitted a disgusted huff. "My chicken is raw."

"Squab," her father corrected. "It's supposed to be pink."

If Lee hadn't been distracted by his flood of memories, both new and old, he might have figured out a way around cutting open the squab. He could come up with some excuse. Dehydration. Nerves. But even as his knife sank into the flesh, even as the crisped skin parted to reveal the glistening, ruby-tinged muscle beneath, all he could manage was to swallow the dread that by this time tomorrow, Emma and Howard would be finally, irrevocably married.

* * *

"That man." Lee's mother put the car in gear and headed toward the stream. The lurching, disconnected feel of the short manual drive from the restaurant to the highway made Lee burp up creme brûlée. It had tasted better the first time around.

"Could you at least wait until we're locked in before you start complaining about them?" Emma suggested.

"Not all of them," Mom said. "Just the father—brag, brag, brag. The rest of the family seemed fine."

"Mom," Emma said firmly, "the road."

Mom pressed her lips together and drove with exaggerated care. Dad hummed to himself as he stared out the window and watched the scenery crawl by. It wasn't that he'd developed a particular knack for tuning out arguments. More like he didn't even notice them.

As the car approached the on-ramp, manual steering

clicked off and the Algorithm took over. A progress bar lit the dash. When Lee was young, very young, before Emma was even born, they'd had a different car. He could still picture it vividly, the body shiny red with tiny flecks of silver, chrome flaking at the handles and rear bumper. Instead of a progress bar, that dashboard had displayed an estimated wait time. Modern cars no longer showed specific times, since wellness psychologists had determined a plain progress bar was less distressing. Maybe, for some people, it was—people like Lee's father, who were basically content. But even from the backseat, Lee could tell his mother was running through calculations in her mind, attempting to determine exactly how long it would take the Algorithm to pull them into traffic.

"Howard's mother seemed nice enough," Mom said.

It was a conciliatory attempt. Even so, Emma snapped back, "Until she chipped her tooth on a piece of buckshot."

"Good thing we went with the chicken for the wedding," Dad declared with the full force of his optimism.

Mom focused on the progress bar.

Emma glared out the window.

Lee wondered if it was possible his father hadn't realized that a single pink-meated, buckshot-peppered, gape-cavitied squab probably cost more than a freezer-load of ordinary chicken. Had the point somehow sailed entirely over his head that not only had the groom's family upstaged the wedding with the elaborate rehearsal dinner, but they'd basked in the satisfaction?

The progress bar dwindled, faster now as the Algorithm's calculations sped, and soon the car clicked onto the highway to begin its smooth glide toward home. It had been years, maybe decades, since an accident occurred on a highway, so usually once Lee felt that click, he'd allow his stomach to unclench. But not tonight. The tension in the car was thick enough to cut with one of the innumerable silver knives pointing every which way in the world's most ostentatious place setting. Everyone was on edge. Everyone but Dad, who had resumed his tuneless humming.

Lee let his hand drop to the seat beside his sister's so the edges of their pinkies brushed together. It was a light touch, but so much more. A reminder of the most solemn promises they'd made—and kept—through the course of their lives. Don't tell Mom and Dad I broke the tail off the ceramic rooster jar. Don't tell them I wet the bed...again. Don't tell them I called Ms. Murray a bitch (she deserved it). Don't tell them I punched that little creep Eddie Marone and made him cry (he *really* deserved it). Don't tell, ever. Promise me. Pinky swear.

By the time they started creeping into the Taxable District to spend their Saturday mornings at the second-hand bookstore, the pinky swear was unnecessary. Childish. And besides, they both shared the guilt, so they were equally invested in keeping their explorations to themselves.

All those secrets, all those years. All of it came flooding back to Lee. Emma could tell him what she was thinking about the rehearsal...about Howard, though she hadn't yet said a word about what she truly thought. His gentle probings were met with vague reassurance. The Algorithm said they were a perfect match, so what's the big deal? Nothing to worry about. Everyone got married, and everyone married their Algorithm pick. No use stressing out over it.

Except she *was* stressed out. People didn't cry hard enough that the sound carried through the walls when tears of joy were being shed. Maybe Lee couldn't do much about the wedding, but he was at least willing to be supportive. He nudged Emma's little finger and offered her a sympathetic look. Except Emma didn't even see it. She glanced down sadly at their side-by-side fingers, sighed, then pulled her hand away and settled it on her lap.

4

THE WALLS WERE NOT particularly thin. Lee's family lived in a newer home, over 83% recycled composite, smallish but sturdy. Three compact bedrooms, two baths—and, according to Dad, a lot easier to clean than those sprawling Mid-Mod revivals over by Hale Creek.

Lee pressed his ear to the wall his bedroom shared with Emma's. He hadn't anticipated her lack of reaction in the car. But what could he expect? The last time he heard her crying, he'd done nothing. Nothing! Roman would have done...something. Lee wasn't sure exactly what, but he couldn't imagine Roman fretting over it with his mouth shut. Unfortunately, now that Lee was prepared to dash over to the next room with offers of hugs and condolences and a shoulder to cry on, his eager ear was met with nothing but silence.

He glanced at the clock. It was late. But Emma couldn't possibly be asleep yet. Could she? He debated for several long minutes whether or not his presence would be a nuisance, then finally decided he'd be haunted by his inaction forever if he squandered his last chance at talking to Emma before the wedding. He crept into the hall. A sliver of light shone from beneath her closed bedroom door. Heartened by the fact that at least he wouldn't be waking her, Lee knocked.

Emma opened the door a crack. "What?"

Lee's mouth worked. Since when did he have a hard time figuring out what to say to his own sister? "Just... checking."

"On what?"

"On you." Lee almost asked if she was okay. Rude, but effectively succinct. However, he suspected that unlike Roman, he couldn't quite carry off such a bold question without tanking the entire conversation. "In case you wanted to talk. About anything."

"Not really. Why? Do you?"

"Well, yeah."

"About what?"

"About tomorrow." Lee's voice faltered. He cleared his throat. "About everything."

"Seriously?" Emma glanced at her clock. "Now?"

Lee's heart sank, and he felt his face screw up.

Emma sighed and opened her door wide. "Okay, okay. Since when are you such a big, sentimental dork?"

"Since everything stopped making sense," Lee murmured, though he suspected it was more than that, and maybe today was the first time certain puzzle pieces actually clicked together.

Normally he would have sat on Emma's bed, but her gift from Mom was currently there, a handmade wedding quilt. It wasn't spread reverently, as it would be on a double bed, an adult bed, but instead it was heaped in a pile at the foot of the narrow mattress. Navy and white—the wedding colors. Not turquoise. Not coral.

Their mother had sourced the fabric for months. She took her quilting as seriously as most folks took the evening news, and for her it would have been a travesty to simply purchase the material at a fabric store. She made "scrap" quilts, so in her mind, even fabric made from recycled fiber violated the spirit. Lee wasn't quite sure how she'd managed to save the correct bits of old clothing all these years when the wedding colors had only been settled on a year and a half ago. But there was a snippet of the sundress Emma had worn to kindergarten. Lee remembered how the skirt would flare when she twirled. She spun and spun, giggling, until she took a few crooked steps and collapsed to the ground. He wished his mother had used the part of the skirt with the stubborn grass stain on it. More memories there. But he supposed if he wanted to express such strong opinions on the fabric choice, he'd need to take up quilting himself.

There was a piece of a cloth napkin Lee hadn't seen in years. And there was a bit of ribbon Emma had won the year she'd conquered every local spelling bee (before she deemed the spelling circuit "vestigial" and dropped the whole thing just as quickly as she'd picked it up.) Most of the fabrics, though, Lee couldn't quite place.

It was possible he hadn't paid enough attention, but it was more likely those scraps didn't hold his family's precious memories at all. There was only so much storage space in their tiny composite house, and only a few token items could have been saved. Most of the fabric would have been sourced from a specialty craft store. The skill of Taxable District trash-pickers was legendary. In the three semesters Lee's studies had focused on the etymology of phrases, he'd done a philosophical analysis on the old idiom that Native Americans used every part of the buffalo. He had a hard time picturing what, exactly, anyone could do with a huge rotting carcass. And yet the phrase resonated with meaning. After all, a skilled trash-picker could turn a refuse pile into a viable stream of income.

Artisanal recycled materials were big business, and they were incredibly labor intensive. Scavenging scraps and rags was only the first step. The fabrics were then thoroughly cleaned and disinfected, pressed, cut into neat squares, and bundled into stacks of various weights and color schemes. Were they more costly than machine-made yardage? Of course. But quilts were a labor of love, a medium of memory, so ideally the fabric going into them would be just as special as the construction.

Lee hefted the quilt—it was heavier than it looked—and attempted to fold it. His knuckles brushed the walls on either side of the room. "How did you know?" he asked.

"Know what?"

"What your wedding colors should be?"

"Uh...I dunno. I just picked some."

"It was that easy for you?"

"Well, sure. I like blue and white. Who doesn't?" Maybe someone who'd choose turquoise and coral in a centerpiece that could have been programmed to glow any color at all. "Look, I know Mom and I have been getting into it lately, but we're just stressed out. There's the ceremony, the reception, the move. It's like white-knuckling it while she's trying to get to the on-ramp without hitting something. After that, it's all highway."

"Maybe what you need is to blow off some steam."

"No," Emma said. "What I need to do is finish packing."

"At the Bonfires."

Emma bit back a reply and studied Lee more closely.

"How much did you have to drink tonight?"

"Only two vodka sours." They hadn't tasted anything like the drink Roman had concocted in the kitchen, either. And they'd churned in his stomach too forcibly to allow him to down any more, though he'd sorely wished he could cultivate a better buzz. "That was hours ago. I'm not drunk. I just thought it would be...fun."

"The *Bonfires*...fun. What would we do for an encore—spray-paint some graffiti? Steal a car? Kill a hobo?"

"It's not like that. There's music."

"You don't even know where it is. It's not like stopping at the mall. There's no fixed address with a fancy sign between the McDonald's and the Starbucks that says *Bonfires*."

"I thought we'd start at Cat and Canary and go from there." They'd been sneaking off to the used bookstore for so many years, they could get there blindfolded. So finding the Bonfires from there, how hard could it be? Big glowy thing by the river....

"What are you thinking, Lee?" Emma couldn't have sounded more exasperated if she tried. "I practically had to bribe you to take me there—and that was during the day. This time of night? They'd skin us alive."

"No they wouldn't."

"Sure they would. We don't belong there. We're lucky Mr. Babcock even tolerated us hanging around the bookstore as much as he did."

What was she talking about? Lee might not know much about business—it was one of the few things he had absolutely no desire to study—but he and Emma were paying customers. "Maybe Babcock doesn't go overboard gushing over our patronage, but it's nothing personal. That's just the way he is."

"Promise me you won't start going there after dark. I can't spare the mental energy to worry about you getting mugged because I'm not there to watch out for you."

"You're talking like you're done with Cat and Canary."

"Lee," Emma said gravely, "the wedding colors, the rehearsal dinner, the quilt...you're a smart guy. I'd hope you can piece together what it all means. That I'm getting married."

Getting married. Not dying. "What are you trying to say? Now you'll never see me again?"

"Don't be so melodramatic. I don't need it—not from you, especially not now."

How had his desire to comfort Emma gone so horribly wrong? If it were any other time, any other situation, he would have made for his room, closed the door, and buried his nose in a book. But while it would be simple enough to retreat, he couldn't bring himself to do it. In the morning, his sister would embark on a whirlwind of wedding activities, and any chance of making sure she didn't want to back out would be lost.

"I'm serious. Let's go to the District. Tonight. Now."

Emma took two corners of the quilt from Lee, backed to the far end of the room, and gave it a shake. The elaborate white and navy checkerboard pattern bowed. She brought her corners together, and Lee did too. Then she walked up to meet him, bringing their ends together. "I'm impressed that you're feeling so adventurous—and, I dunno, maybe if you'd brought it up a few weekends ago, you could've talked me into it. But I'm not going out tonight. I have an incredibly long day tomorrow, and everyone will be taking pictures. I need some sleep."

Lee struggled to find some convincing argument to

counter with, but could only come up with, "Please."

"Some other time. Next month, maybe, once I'm back from the honeymoon and all settled in. We'll plan it."

Next month would be too late. Anytime after the ceremony and the vows and the paperwork would be too damn late. "Aren't you sick of planning? Haven't you had enough of doing what's expected of you? Of playing out this role that someone—or some *thing*—determined for you without ever once checking with you to see if it was something you actually wanted?"

Emma yanked the quilt from his hands, gave it three more hasty, crooked folds, then slammed it onto her bed. Lee might have been the one who'd had an article on metaphor published in Historical Words Journal, but Emma knew him well enough to understand he wasn't really talking about going out with him tonight. "You're nearly thirty, Lee. You don't need your little sister to take you to the Bonfires. If you're so caught up in the idea of going to the District right this very second, go there yourself."

5

THE CAT AND CANARY bookstore looked vastly different at Midnight than it did on a sunny Saturday afternoon. The lights were out. The doors were covered by a metal security grating. And through the window, the used books with all their different colors and shapes and sizes, with their dog-eared pages and velvety, worn corners—this daytime treasure trove—looked more like a teetering pile of junk. But Lee had been sneaking off to Cat and Canary so long, he could find it in the dark. Literally. If there were any doubt, he could make out the hand-painted logo on the glass, with graffiti etched into the cat. A few crooked whiskers, and a squiggle on its haunches that was probably a gang symbol. Next to that was the series of faded stickers that ran down the side of the pane, odd little childish things. Shining suns, apples and lollipops, all of them with cherubic smiling faces.

Lee wasn't sure why graffiti hadn't quite caught on in the Benefit Sector neighborhoods where he spent the majority of his time. Maybe the perfect composite surfaces were impervious to any attempts to mark them. He'd never known a Boomer past Kindergarten age to cover things with stickers, either. But here in the District, everything was simultaneously decaying and adorned. Stickers and graffiti were part of the landscape—along with determined flowering weeds stretching up through the cracks in the old sidewalks, paint peeling to reveal numerous colors and iterations, and jumbles of handbills pasted ten layers deep, advertising various activist groups and social causes.

The word *Bonfires* caught his eye from one of the handbills on the stump of an old utility pole, and he searched for an address. But, no, there wasn't one. Just a photo of a band called Weeping Bubo looking tattooed, hairy and angry. Although there was a date listed—three weeks ago—apparently there was no need to say what time Weeping Bubo would take the stage. Or, for that matter, where the Bonfires even were.

Apparently, if Lee weren't a Benefit Boomer, he would simply know.

Confusion threatened to overwhelm him. It wasn't only that he didn't know where the Bonfires were. (How hard *could* they be to find?) It was that nothing else made sense anymore. How was it that instead of being relieved that he was offering support, Emma was angry? And how could Roman's kiss have lingered on his lips despite the grease-coating they'd gotten from that obscene squab?

Lee shut his eyes, took a deep breath and squared his shoulders. He knew where the river was. And so he struck off in that direction.

One of the many ways in which Lee worried he'd stick out like the proverbial sore thumb was the fact that he was on foot. But District streets were nothing like the Benefit Sector. They'd been laid out in an era when there was no traffic algorithm and people manually drove their cars everywhere, crashing into each other and mowing down pedestrians. There were a few modern automobile tracks that led to the highway here, but nowhere near as numerous as in Lee's neighborhood. More people rode bicycles—and more people walked. Even this late at night. No one noticed the fact that he was on foot. No one cared.

Before long, he made out something that didn't sound much like a song, though the distinct squall of an electric guitar carried over the top of the muted rumble. The river was in sight. The sound guided him until the glow of the fire came into view. Other people were heading that way, too, but they didn't look like the vicious mob he'd seen on the news. They just looked like people.

Which wasn't to say he'd ever mistake one of them for a Benefit Boomer. Only that they weren't currently pounding one another with loose bricks or scraps of lumber. The scattering of people became a freeform crowd, and Lee realized he was part of it, everyone strolling in the direction of the river, and the music, and the big glowy thing. His heart pounded, but not entirely with fear. While the Bonfires felt nothing at all like the violent newscasts, joining the Taxable District crowd was the most thrilling thing he'd ever done... aside from kissing Roman.

As the ground angled down toward the riverbank, the view of the band and the fire was blocked by a tangled stand of weed trees. Lee allowed himself to flow with the crowd. There was a well-worn footpath he would have totally missed in the dark. But it was easy enough to focus on the couple in front of him, a twenty-something man and woman holding hands, and allow his feet to find the path without the help of his experience or his eyes.

He shuffled through the trees, not sure what he would find on the other side, and not caring. Whatever the experience turned out to be, it was already leaps and bounds better than the rehearsal dinner. And then the path turned, and the landscape blossomed with sound and fire.

The sound resolved itself into a beat. On a makeshift stage, three guitar players lunged in time, swinging their long, tangled hair in great, synchronized swoops while the drummer flailed. In counterpoint, the massive fire in front of them leapt randomly, too wild to be contained by something as contrived as rhythm. The crowd had formed a ragged circle around the fire, mostly men, surging around it clockwise in broad, lurching steps. Some of them shoved and jostled at one another as they went, but in person, the shoving looked more playful than violent. When one of the guys lost his footing, three others scooped him up and dragged him back into the flow. A row of spectators stood firm in front of the band, facing the stage, bobbing their heads and swinging their hair. But most of the crowd allowed themselves to be carried around the fire by the current.

Not everyone got close enough to be pulled into the tide—close enough to feel their eardrums ache from the roar of the amplifiers, or be singed by a wayward ember. Farther from the stage, some people watched the band, swaying slightly or nodding their heads to the rhythm. Some weren't even paying attention to the show, and talked in clusters instead, gesticulating and laughing.

And some couples at the very fringe of the gathering were kissing.

When Lee stopped to stare, the crowd he'd been part of simply flowed around him, a lot like the men circling the fire. It wasn't the fear of being physically hurt that was holding him back, it was the fear that he wouldn't be able to figure out how to fit in. But it wasn't as if he'd find Roman by hiding in the trees. He steeled himself, and he pressed on.

Even if Roman was in that churn of bodies around the fire, Lee suspected it would be pretty tough to find him even by jumping in. But occasionally someone would stagger out from the fray, sweaty and winded. So finding Roman was just a matter of patience.

While he was waiting for more guys to tumble out of the circle, he could also scan the groups of people who were just hanging out. Unfortunately, without a flashlight, he had to get really close to see them. And getting close enough to make out the partiers' features also exposed him. He approached a cluster of men and woman who were talking and laughing. They fell silent and stared.

"Sorry," he said, though they couldn't have heard it over the band, and veered away. He skirted the next group more cautiously. It was surprising how many District guys had the same raw-boned, angular build as Roman. Lee tried focusing on the hair, but soon realized that Roman could have spiked up his sleek black hair for the occasion, or he could be wearing a hat. Plus, unless he was wearing something that looked exactly like his catering uniform, the chance of picking him out by silhouette alone wasn't just slim, it was infinitesimal.

Not only that, but Lee could tell that even though he was trying to keep some distance between himself and the audience, people were starting to stare. He shoved his hands in his pockets and tried to pull in on himself, but it was no use. Unless he'd spontaneously developed the ability to turn invisible, he was going to be seen.

He had his attention on a particularly threatening-looking group of District dwellers in leather and spikes and chains when he blundered directly into someone—a young woman in tattered black denim with eyes ringed in thick purple liner. She might have seemed threatening, if her high pigtails didn't remind him of a five-year-old Emma.

Lee automatically reached out to steady her. "I'm sorry."

When Lee's fingertips brushed her shoulder, she raked him up and down with her gaze, and she smirked. "Don't be," she yelled into his ear. "That's the most action I've seen all night. So, tell me...what's a nice boy like you doing in a place like this?"

No doubt he wouldn't have been more obvious if he had *Boomer* written across his forehead. But the woman didn't seem angry with him for being there, just curious, so he figured he might as well ask for help. He leaned in and yelled over the feedback, "I'm looking for Roman Sharp. Do you know him?"

The question earned him a raised eyebrow and a lingering once-over. Pigtails didn't answer. She gave him a shrug, then turned away, slipped into the crowd, and disappeared into the flickering darkness.

Strange. But at least it gave him an idea. The District women seemed willing enough to talk to him, more than the women would've been in the Benefit Sector— and although they might be just as likely as the District men to pull a knife or knee him in the groin, they didn't *feel* nearly as threatening.

"Do you know Roman Sharp?" he found himself

asking, again and again, pressing his mouth to dozens of women's ears as intimately as a lover. Personal space was different at the Bonfires, and not only for the men knocking each other down and then scooping their fallen comrades right back into the fray. The women leaned into Lee. Not only was he obviously harmless, but he probably looked like an easy mark, too. Mr. Babcock at Cat and Canary might not have been the chattiest guy, but early on, he'd made it known that Lee would soon find himself without a wallet if he insisted on parading around the District with a billfold in his back pocket. Given the number of times by the Bonfire Lee felt hands fleeting across the back of his jeans, he figured plenty of other dumb Boomers must not have had the benefit of that advice.

How many people were there, a few hundred? Not many more than he expected at his sister's wedding. Tomorrow. He shoved that thought aside and worked his way around the crowd, finding the ebb and flow of the music, figuring out when songs would end so his question was more likely to actually be heard. Eventually, when he was fairly sure nobody was going to stab him, Lee tried asking a few men if they knew Roman Sharp. Nobody did.

At the far end of the gathering, an area the size of the meeting hall's kitchen was sectioned off with a makeshift fence of crude wooden stakes and rope. The cluster of people inside was thick. They weren't dancing or shoving each other around. They weren't really paying much attention to the band at all. Maybe Roman was there.

Lee joined the straggling line of people being let one by one into the special pen. A man sat on a stool at a gap in the fence with a bucket on his lap, collecting admission. Lee wasn't keen on pulling out his wallet at the Bonfires, but he'd picked through the rest of the crowd, and if Roman was anywhere, it would be inside that special area.

He pulled out some smaller bills when no one was looking, then shoved his wallet back beneath his button-down, into his T-shirt pocket. The line moved forward, faster now. As each person dropped in their payment, the guy on the stool—a very big guy, bald, with lots of spikes on his leather vest—checked the bucket first, then nodded the person through. Usually. But once he made a "more" gesture, and the guy in line had to cough up extra money to get in.

Lee wadded together a few bills and hoped it would be enough. Before long it was his turn at the bucket, and he did his best to look casual, to look like he knew what he was doing, like he knew what things cost in the District, things other than dog-eared used books. He tried very, very hard to look like he belonged.

Stilling his face into what he hoped was a mask of indifference, Lee dropped in his wad of cash and prepared to go inside. The song wound down and the music stopped, all but a thin whine of feedback and the sizzling reverberation of a cymbal. And in the sudden silence, the big bald guy in leather and spikes bellowed, "What the fuck am I supposed to do with this?"

6

Too little? Too much? Lee steeled himself and looked into the bucket.

The interior of the rim had been decorated with stickers, District style. And inside, there was his money-wad. Sitting right on top. Not on a pile of cash, but on a pile of random objects. Coffee packets and batteries and lipstick and mints. The only thing that even vaguely resembled cash was the scattering of shuttle tokens.

He pawed through his pockets to see what he could possibly come up with. Some change (useless.) A crumpled note containing a few phrases for his speech (also useless.) And a comb.

He dropped in the comb.

The bald man looked into the bucket, then back up at Lee, and mouthed the word, "What?" He shoved the bucket into Lee's chest with a scowl that conveyed, loud and clear, *Stop fucking around.*

But Lee had nothing else to give.

"I'm sorry," he said, for what felt like the hundredth time that night, then held up his hands and backed away. Or he tried to. The line behind him had grown restless, and suddenly it felt like people were pressed all around him. District residents. Who were a lot more intimidating than they'd seemed a minute ago.

A pair of hands fell on his shoulders, and Lee knew with a striking clarity that he should never have come. Maybe people hardly ever got killed at the Bonfires. But sometimes, they did.

He steeled himself, fully prepared to be dragged away, beaten, kicked, and thrown in the river, but instead he was only shoved aside so a hand could thrust into the bucket and drop something. Lee stared down stupidly at the huge handful of sugar packets that now covered his unwanted money...sugar packets printed *Howard and Emma* in fancy script, with tomorrow's date beneath the names. The scary bald man nodded, and Lee let himself be dragged into the roped-off pen.

When the hands spun him around and he found himself staring into Roman's dark eyes, he suspected the whole thing was actually some sort of dream...or at least a delusion. Either he'd boozed himself to sleep after the rehearsal dinner and was having disturbing vodka-dreams, or he was currently sinking to the bottom of the river, where his dying brain offered up a final longed-for image to take with him to the great beyond.

"Seriously," Roman shouted over the music, "a comb?"

"I'm sorry."

Roman gave Lee's shoulders a squeeze, then took him by the hand and led him to the far end of the enclosure. The music shifted as his angle to the amplifiers changed, and now the guitar and vocals ebbed, leaving mostly bass guitar, thumping steadily, punctuated by the rap of a snare. They pushed through a cluster of people. In the corner behind a folding table, a gray-haired woman was pouring drinks from a gallon jug, filtered through a scrap of cheesecloth fastened over the jug's neck. The cups were a mishmash of shapes and sizes, some teacups, some highball glasses, some jelly jars. All-you-can-drink? It appeared so. And the people crowded around the table were intent on getting as much return as possible on whatever they'd tossed in the bucket.

Roman let go of Lee's hand, grabbed a drink for himself and shoved another drink at him. All around them, people swarmed to the table, snatching up drinks as fast as the woman could pour. From the corner of his eye, Lee watched a man drain the last of his drink and put his World's Greatest Dad coffee mug back on the table. The woman refilled it and set it out with all the others.

Roman tapped the rim of his plastic tumbler to Lee's and shouted, "To your health." That toast actually predated the plague...but even if Roman could hear Lee imparting that bit of trivia over the roar of the band, it was unlikely he would've been terribly impressed. Because what good was knowing all about language when, in fact, you had no clue what anything truly meant? Lee met his eyes and tipped back his drink— and very nearly spit it back out. The overpowering flavor was mustiness, verging on rot. Beneath that, the burn of alcohol. And maybe a hint of fermented orange.

Lee gagged. Roman nodded sympathetically and yelled over the music, "Orange Malt. It's an acquired taste." He finished what was in his glass, snagged two more cups from the table, and motioned with his chin for Lee to move to a spot on the perimeter that was slightly less mobbed. Lee found a gap in the crowd.

Roman came and stood beside him and drank, watching Lee intently over the rim of his canning jar. Lee took small sips from his tumbler. It wasn't quite as bad if he was careful not to breathe through his nose.

The song that had been thundering along meandered to a stop. "So, you showed up," Roman said in the relative silence, though he still needed to raise his voice over the weave of a dozen other conversations.

"Here I am." Lee's sister was right, he was a big dork. He hid a wince with a sip of his drink. Which was growing on him, except for that undertone of rot.

"There you are." Roman knocked back the rest of his second drink, pocketed the cup, and started the third. He shook his head. "I didn't think you'd—"

Whatever else he'd been about to say was cut off by the sharp, staccato attack of a snare with a bass riff rumbling along beneath it. *He didn't think I'd what?* Have the courage to find the bonfire? Not surprising. Every step of the way, Lee had fought the impulse to turn around and run back home. Heck, he was still struggling with the urge to flee.

Much of the nuance of language lay in the inflection and tone. In other words, it's not what you say, but how you say it. There were so many things to say, but the meaning would be lost if he shouted them into Roman's ear. How long did a song last? Three minutes? Four? It seemed like he'd been waiting forever for the band to wrap up whatever it was they were churning through. But every time he was sure the song was coming to an end, they launched into another verse.

He should have used the pause to gather his wits and think of something to say that wouldn't make him sound ridiculous. But he'd finally found Roman. As Lee watched him looking back with a smile playing at the corners of his eyes, words drained away. Roman hadn't done anything special to his hair after all. It was still a glossy black fringe that slanted across his forehead and tickled the top of his cheekbone. And Roman still felt no need to brush it off his face. He'd changed into a leather biker jacket and black jeans, but they didn't look much different on him than the catering uniform. He was still a harsh black silhouette, all angles and planes.

Finally, the song ended, and Roman spared Lee the discomfort of trying to figure out what to say. "What made you decide to come tonight?"

A better question might have been how Lee managed to overcome the fear of ending up at the bottom of the river, though it sounded appealingly calm and restful compared to the anticipation of enduring Emma's wedding. "No idea. When we talk, I feel like I don't know anything about anything."

"So ignorance isn't really bliss."

But it was. Lee didn't know much about economics, other than the fact that it was nowhere near as interesting as language. Now that he saw his knowledge was cobbled together from presumptions and propaganda, he suspected that ignorance was, if not blissful, at least a lot more comfortable than the feeling of his reality turning upside down and inside out.

"Whatever the reason," Roman said, "I'm really glad you did."

The band churned into another song. Never taking his eyes off Lee, Roman tipped back his third drink, draining it. Lee attempted to follow suit, but only managed to swallow about half of his. Roman pulled the tumbler from his grasp, finished it off, pressed his mouth to Lee's ear and said, "Let's get out of here."

7

THERE WAS MORE THAN one footpath through the trees. Lee didn't have an entire mob to follow, though, only one man, but the simple contact of palm to palm pulled at him as strongly as the surge of the crowd. As the trees grew thicker, the music's character changed as distinct elements were muffled, and soon it sounded like more of a rhythmic throb with the hint of a melody threading through it. As Lee threaded through the trees in the dark, he became a melody, drawn along by the rhythm, the foundation, of his tenuous connection with Roman.

He hadn't heard this particular song before, so he couldn't quite sing along—but he was willing to listen.

Roman's feet found a path, and soon they emerged on a typical District street. When Roman let go of his hand, Lee didn't know what to do with it anymore. He settled for shoving it awkwardly in his pocket. Roman gestured toward a side street that led deeper into the warren of old apartments as he glanced at Lee. Lee nodded and hoped he looked even remotely casual. They headed in.

"You looked pretty spooked after I kissed you," Roman

said. "I thought maybe I'd pegged you wrong after all."

"That depends on what you were thinking."

"Figured you were either one of those introverted loner intellectual-types who doesn't want to deal with a wife—or you were gay, or at least curious, and didn't want to drag all your baggage into an arranged marriage."

Lee trudged along the cracked sidewalk. "I'm not a loner," he said. "I like spending time with my family."

In the distance, a song ended with a squeal of feedback. The gravelly sound of an untethered car rolling by filled the silence.

"But you are gay."

People in vintage TV shows were gay. Just like they had huge houses and voted for political officials, and they got married and divorced and married again, and had great scads of kids with multiple partners, or maybe decided to have no children and live alone, possibly with cats.

As for Lee? He'd gone through the motions of sex ed to make sure he kept up his GPA, and he'd played along with the snigger and swagger of his classmates without really understanding the allure. But the encounter in the kitchen broke open something inside he hadn't even realized he'd been suppressing. He shrugged. "Guess I'd avoided thinking about it until today."

"I was so sure I'd screwed everything up, I didn't realize what was going on tonight. Someone told me a guy was looking for me, and it never even occurred to me it was you. People kept snagging me, though, telling me some guy was asking around. My debts are settled and I'm not in the market for any batteries or pills, so I even thought about leaving early, taking off and avoiding some kind of misunderstanding...until my friend

Roxy mentioned that this guy had a Boomer accent and face like an angel, and it all clicked. If I didn't hurry up and take you home, she said, somebody else would." Roman paused in front of a clapboard three-story walkup and fit an old metal key into the security grating. "You don't have to spend the night with me, y'know."

Oh, but he did. Lee didn't say so out loud. It wasn't worth arguing—he'd come too far to leave now. "I can't stop thinking about that kiss," he said. And then he felt like an idiot.

At least until Roman slid his gaze to Lee and said, "That makes two of us."

Lee didn't know what to do with himself, but it didn't matter. Roman swung him around, pressed him into the security grating and kissed him hard. He'd been replaying the kitchen kiss all day, so many times that he knew it inside and out. Enough that he thought he knew everything there could be to know about a kiss. But he was wrong. This kiss had a different character, as a word might have a different shade of meaning, depending on its context and tone, and the relationship of the speaker to the listener. This kiss was solid enough to hold decisions. What, exactly, Roman had decided, Lee couldn't know. But it embodied his own choice to come to the District and find Roman. And it held his resolve to see how the night would play out.

Out on the street, voices rose and fell. People fighting, or maybe laughing. Roman broke the kiss to glance back over his shoulder, then nudged Lee aside and pulled open the security grate.

Lee didn't think he had any particular expectations of Roman's house, but apparently he had. Not things like decor, or even size. But that the rooms would serve the same basic functions that they did in his own house. Instead, the main room looked more like Cat and Canary, with shelves of items and mismatched furniture, bureaus stacked several high. He had to duck three bicycles hanging from the ceiling on his way through the maze.

Roman pointed out a door and said, "Bathroom," and though Lee didn't really need to go, he figured he should at least check and make sure there wasn't something weird involved that he'd need to learn. Maybe he'd always presumed things were basically the same in the Taxable District. But they weren't. Not at all.

The bathroom walls were crowded with shelves. Three toothbrushes protruded from a cup on the sink. Multiple towels hung from the walls. But at least he recognized the fixtures—hopefully. He checked the shower for "bathtub gin," but thankfully, he found nothing more than scrubbies and soaps and shampoos.

"Want to shower?" Roman said. "You won't catch anything. Promise."

You won't catch anything? And here Lee'd been scandalized by *How are you?* "No. I just...wondered."

"How many people live here? You only need to ask. Three. We're housemates—totally platonic."

It would never have occurred to Lee the relationship might be otherwise.

Roman led him to a door and opened it. Lee had been expecting an actual room, and again his expectations were challenged. It wasn't a room. It was a closet. Literally. He could tell by the old coat hooks in the wall. But it had been inset with a lofted bed above a desk. "Don't worry, we'll fit," Roman said. There was a bookshelf inset on the side of the desk. He climbed it like a ladder, then turned himself around and offered Lee a hand.

They did fit. Barely. If they kept their knees slightly bent. In other circumstances, Lee might have wanted to close the door for privacy, but he was worried they'd both suffocate.

They lay facing one another, Roman on the outside where, hopefully, he wouldn't fall out. He tucked his forearm under his head and said, "You can still bail, y'know. I wouldn't blame you."

"Why would I?"

"Now you've had a good look at me. A Tax Rat's not half as threatening when he's out of his element. But here...."

"Don't say that!"

"Why not? Everyone else does."

"Not in my house," Lee insisted. When Emma was eight, she'd picked up the slur at school and showed it off at the dinner table. Mom parked her in the corner for the rest of the night. And Dad didn't even sneak her a dessert.

Roman probably thought Lee's family was like Howard's, a bunch of arrogant, ostentatious blow-hards. And, really, why wouldn't he? Compared with this apartment, their modest composite home was a mansion. Lee suspected he couldn't really convey what he felt with words, especially since he couldn't quite find a word for his emotions—fear and shame and exuberance and longing all mingled together—so instead he pulled his shirt over his head.

Vintage. There were usually a few odds and ends for sale at Cat and Canary other than books. Bits of clothing. Knick knacks. Flowers. He told his mother it was the purple and blue paisley that had caught his eye, but really, wearing it was nothing more than a silly attempt to blend in.

"You almost passed for District in that shirt," Roman said.

"But I didn't." He'd never realized he had an accent.

"Doesn't matter. You're here." Roman peeled off his own top, then skimmed his fingertips over Lee's bare arm. Lee shivered. "I was serious about that shower offer, y'know. Real sex isn't nearly as antiseptic as what you're used to."

"No. I don't want some sanitized version of reality." For once.

Roman traced a path down Lee's chest, kindly ignoring his squirming, and said, "I like the smell of woodsmoke, actually." He pressed his mouth to Lee's ear, inhaled deeply, and sighed. The tickle of breath against his earlobe caused a shockwave to ripple through Lee, from his scalp to his clenched toes. "Scent is linked to memory—and I always have a good time at the Bonfires."

Lee pressed his nose to Roman's hair. It did smell like woodsmoke, and so much more. It smelled like a real person under there, someone who wanted to be together for whatever complex human reasons he had, and not because he was obligated to teach Lee about the ins and outs—literally—of sexuality. Lee had been lectured, drilled and quizzed on touch, yet now it felt overwhelming to decide where to begin. He slipped his hand around Roman's bare waist, not with any real strategy, but simply because that was where his hand naturally fell. It brought them closer, chest to chest and thigh to thigh. Lee walked his fingers across the flat hard plane just above the tailbone, and Roman moaned against his cheek. It was nothing at all like the calm feedback his teacher would have uttered. He dragged his fingers higher. Sinew, muscle, bone—scent, touch and sound—all of it was strange. Nothing like his sex ed teacher. Nothing like the woman waiting for him to trigger the Algorithm.

Roman arched against him, and the bulges in their pants butted together. He asked Lee, "You're still into this, right?"

"Yes."

"You're so quiet, it's hard to tell."

That was probably for the best. The only thing Lee could think to say was that he was sorry—and according to Ms. Carmichael, apologies should be kept to a minimum in the bedroom. "I'm into it."

Roman caught his wrist. He shoved Lee's hand down the front of his tattered black jeans. "You sure?"

The only thing Lee was sure of was that he really, really wanted Roman to stop grilling him about what they were doing—and that he had no idea what his hand was encountering, just that things were fleshy and hot and surprisingly hairy behind that zipper.

Of course they were. This wasn't sex ed. It was reality.

"Lee?"

"Don't second-guess me. I'm into it." Lee worked his fingers around the base of Roman's erect penis and straightened it inside the jeans so it pointed toward his waistband. Roman gasped. His breath was hot against Lee's neck. Lee took a deep breath, then wriggled and wrenched his way down to the lower half of the bed while Roman uttered small sounds of approval. Lee only hit his head once. Maybe twice. When he looked up, Roman cupped his cheek.

From the low angle, Roman's expression was unreadable, but Lee was fairly sure he couldn't have done anything wrong yet. He unzipped Roman's fly and tugged the jeans open. Sparse light leaking through the warren of living room boxes lit the contour of a vein starkly against the hard shaft. Roman reached down, grasped himself, and swiped his thumb over the slit. "Before you go down, check for wayward pubes, like this. The back of your throat will thank you."

An image of the naked squab sprang to mind. Lee shoved it aside. He sized up the glans and wet his lips.

"Take your time. Don't gag yourself."

"Could you...stop talking to me like a teacher?"

"Oh. Okay." Roman gave himself a few more strokes while the corners of his eyes creased in a subtle smile. "Then get to it, prettyboy, and suck my big, hard dick."

The most important sex organ is the brain. Lee had never understood the overused phrase until that very moment. But when Roman spoke to him like that— prodding an erection toward his face—a giddy sensation swept over him in a wave so intense it felt more like a tumble from the top bunk, than arousal. Roman grabbed him by the hair and shoved in. It took a few strokes before Lee realized that Roman wasn't actually holding his head very hard...and that he should probably start sucking.

"Mm, yeah," Roman breathed. Lee felt his own testicles shift. "Sweet mouth. So damn hot...." Roman set the pace and the depth—not terribly deep, nowhere near as deep as his female classmates had boasted about taking it—but between the writhing and the hair-tugging, the charred bonfire scent and the dirty phrases uttered in that taboo District accent, Lee realized precisely what he should have been fantasizing about all those times he struggled to the point of rawness to finish.

He allowed himself to steal a caress, fingers creeping over the planes of Roman's heaving belly and the smattering of wiry chest hair. He went deeper, sucked harder, and Roman's back arched off the thin mattress. "Yeah...like that...." The words weren't dirty in themselves, but the way they rode the broken edge of desire was everything. "I'm so close."

Already? Lee grunted his encouragement.

"Fuck, oh fuck...where should I come—your pretty face? Your hot mouth?"

Lee had no idea. His head was spinning and his mouth had a salty, hard penis jammed in deep. His reply wasn't even a word, but he supposed it didn't matter. Roman's ejaculate not only spurted against his soft palate and the back of his tongue, it christened him from eyelash to chin to chest. Roman sagged, mouth open, arm dangling over the side of the bunk while his chest heaved and his spent penis softened on his belly. Lee felt a bead of semen roll sluggishly over his collarbone to the hollow of his throat.

After several deep, deliberate breaths, Roman opened his eyes. He looked a lot less threatening with his face flushed and his jeans around his knees. He thumbed some tackiness from Lee's cheek and said, "That was amazing."

Thank you was no more appropriate between the sheets than *I'm sorry*, at least according to Ms. Carmichael. Lee shrugged.

"C'mon back up here, it's my turn to make your toes curl."

One way to ensure your wife is not faking her orgasm is to check for the flexion of her toes. Lee swallowed. And swallowed again.

"Lee?"

A mutually satisfying experience is critical to the success of your marriage.

"Hey...Lee. You okay?"

"Yes," Lee replied, too quickly.

"Y'know, if you stay all scrunched down at the foot of the mattress, I can't reach your dick."

Lee tried to focus on the playful lilt of Roman's voice, but all he could hear was Ms. Carmichael. Factual. Unassuming. And excruciatingly patient.

Communication is the key to building marital trust.

Lee's heart was pounding, not with some illicit thrill anymore, but with panic and dread.

Roman threaded his fingers through Lee's hair, fingertips grazing his scalp, tracing small circles. They stayed that way several long moments, nothing moving but Roman's fingers. When he finally spoke, his voice was so low and gentle, Lee had to strain to hear it. "D'you wanna talk about it?"

"It's the Orange Malt. It's not sitting well."

"Yeah, I probably should've warned you about that. There's a plastic bag in the corner, up by those paperbacks." Roman's eyelids drooped and fluttered, as his hand fell away from Lee's hair. "Try not to hurl on the sheets."

8

THE NAUSEA EXCUSE WAS so flimsy, there was no way it would have flown if Roman hadn't been half asleep. And yet it was the taste of rotten orange homebrew that woke Lee—and the lingering funk was significantly worse the morning after than it had been the night before. His first panicky thought was that if Roman caught a whiff of his breath, he'd be flung into the street. But then he realized he had an awful lot of mattress all to himself.

Normally, Lee could just avoid breathing on people if he needed to divert his morning breath. Now, though, it was entirely possible he'd have a chance to kiss Roman goodbye...and him without a toothbrush. How sad, if the last thing he remembered from this encounter was the fact that his mouth was too vile to coax out one fleeting, final moment of connection. As he pondered the fact that it was just as well he'd left his comb in that bucket since he'd probably just hurt himself trying to brush his teeth with it, an unfamiliar male voice carried through the shelves and stacks and hanging bicycles where the living room should have been. "...it's about time. 'Sall I can say."

And then a woman. "But you could at least close your door. I mean, you fought me tooth and nail for that private bedroom and then you don't close the door."

A laugh. Roman's. "I wasn't that loud."

"You could hear a mouse fart in this place," the man observed.

"Shut the hell up," Roman said affably. "You couldn't hear shit."

The man pitched his voice high and mocking, "Ooh, baby, smoke my salami."

"Damn it, Troy, shut up," the woman said. "You'll make me hurl."

Troy pitched his voice even higher. "La-di-da, I'm *Spike*. I act like such a badass but I toss my cookies at the mere mention of dick."

"I hate you both," she said, matter-of-fact.

The sound of footsteps, and a few jibes Lee didn't quite catch over the sound of clattering plates and shifting furniture, or maybe because his cheeks were blazing so hard they'd diverted the working bloodflow from his eardrums. He located his underwear, his jeans, and slipped into them as quietly as he could.

Out in the apartment, movement settled, and in the pause that followed, Troy said, "But seriously...did I detect an accent?"

"Oh God," said the woman, Spike, especially loud. "You didn't."

Troy said, "Know how you can spot a Boomer? They hammer their plosives like they're building another shopping mall."

"Do you *enjoy* getting hurt?" Spike demanded.

Laughter. Just the men. Then Troy said, "If Roman's kinks were that common, he could shop a little closer to home. But lighten up, this is the only one he actually bagged. So tell me, studly, are they as good in the sack as everyone claims?" More laughter. But only Troy's. "Ruined for normal District guys now?"

"Asshole."

"Hey, hey. Don't be so graphic—I wasn't fishing for specifics."

Spike said, "You know that Boomer's just slumming, right? Using you 'cos he's bored with his perfect Algorithm wife."

"You have no clue what you're talking about. You haven't even met him."

Lee pulled on his shirt. He was dressed now, except for his shoes, which he'd left on the floor outside the closet. He crawled down the bookcase ladder, expecting it to creak and announce his presence. It didn't. He supposed that was for the best. It saved him from having to figure out what he had to say for himself. Funny. When he'd first woken, he thought his problems were as simple as morning breath. Now he was mortified by the sheer fact of his existence. He stepped into his shoes and crept around a bookshelf, glancing in the direction of the voices. A stack of filing cabinets hid the room beyond—a kitchen, judging by the gurgle of running water and the scent of slightly burnt toast.

Home free. Lee planned to slip out while Roman and his friends were occupied with breakfast so no one would be any the wiser. He turned toward the door, and froze. A couch blocked his way. And on the couch, a thin, blue-haired woman with a neck tattoo was curled against the far end, staring up at him in horror. They both froze, eyes locked. In the kitchen, dishes clattered. Lee took a tentative step toward the front door. The woman didn't leap up and stop him, so he took another. And another. He reached for the doorknob.

"So that's how it is?" the woman snapped. Spike. "Not even a goodbye?"

Lee's hand dropped to his side.

Footsteps, then Roman's voice. "Lee, hold on."

Lee couldn't bring himself to look. He remained facing the door, shutting his eyes too. It didn't help. He still wished he was anywhere but there.

Troy said, "Told ya. Sound carries."

"Shut up," Roman snapped. "Both of you." He dropped a hand to Lee's shoulder. Lee flinched. Roman pitched his voice low and gentle, and said, "Don't leave like this."

But Lee wasn't nearly strong enough to stay, brazen and defiant, in a place where he clearly didn't belong. "I'm sorry. I need to go."

"At least have a coffee." Roman saw Lee hesitate, and pressed on. "I already poured it. You don't want it to go to waste."

How was it that someone whose life was as different from his as it could possibly be would know the exact button to push? In Lee's family, *waste* was almost as taboo an utterance as *Tax Rat*. His shoulders sagged in resignation. He could endure his shame for the amount of time it took to drink a single coffee. He had to. He turned and met Roman's gaze, and saw a tenderness there he hadn't noticed back in the banquet hall, or out by the Bonfires. Or maybe it was just that Roman's cynicism paled in comparison to his roommates' cheerful bitterness. He forced a smile and tugged Lee back through the storage warren, past Spike, still gawking from the couch, and into the kitchen.

It hadn't been designed as an eat-in kitchen, but half the shelves were crammed precariously full and the other half had been replaced with a narrow table and three mismatched chairs. A stout, broad-faced man with freckles and multiple lip piercings glanced up from the table as he took a loud slurp of coffee. He blinked, then looked down at his mug. "Oh. Wait a sec. This wasn't for me?"

Roman sighed.

Lee took it as a sign. He wasn't meant to be there. He should never have come. He strode back through the storage room—back past Spike, who was still staring—with Roman right at his heels. "C'mon, Lee, wait a sec. At least let me treat you to breakfast."

Lee paused. It was some sort of test, it had to be. To see if he would insist on paying the bill? To see if he'd try to pay the check with a comb? *Joke's on them. My comb is somewhere in a bucket full of sugar packets and pocket lint.*

Roman wadded the back of Lee's shirt in his hand, pulled himself close, and pressed his lips to the nape of Lee's neck. "C'mon," he murmured, and a shiver coursed down Lee's spine, almost tantalizing enough to cut through his mortification. "I don't want you to remember our date like this."

Well. That sealed it. Maybe the housemates thought he was a jerk. But if he insisted on storming off in hurt indignation now, after what Roman said, he would actually *be* one. "Okay."

"Two minutes," Roman said, and disappeared into the maze of shelves and boxes, heading for his lofted closet.

Lee stood in the single clear spot—and the only reason there weren't piles of stuff there was so people could open the door. He could have sat on the couch, he supposed, if the other person on it wasn't staring at him like he was covered in buboes and coughing up blood.

Spike was crammed in the corner, cross-legged, with a full basket in her lap. At first Lee thought she was doing something with berries, cleaning them in preparation for whatever arcane process turned fruit into alcohol. But then she dipped her hand in and the tiny round things in the basket clattered together. Beads. She picked up a handful and scrubbed them with a wire brush.

Lee offered an attempt at civil conversation. "What are you doing?"

"Distressing." She scrubbed harder. "Vintage items sell better than brand new ones, but there's only so many antique necklaces that can be pulled apart so crafty Boomers can feel self-important about stringing them back together."

Distressing was right. Lee hoped his mother never found out her quilt scraps weren't recycled after all, just made to look that way.

He stood there awkwardly while Spike scrubbed, and eventually said, "I'm not married."

She scowled and scrubbed more intently.

"I'm not," he insisted. "I'm still in school."

"Studying what?"

"Language."

She scoffed. "Sounds to me like you've got a decent handle on the whole talking thing. How much longer is it gonna take you?"

Lee didn't dignify that observation with a response. He silently watched as she sifted through the clacking beads, grabbed another handful and scrubbed. Then she picked up a scrap of sandpaper and buffed them with grit.

"So you live in the dorms?" she asked.

A dorm room would've been a luxury his parents

were far too thrifty to consider, but Lee suspected his idea of thrift was preposterous in the Taxable District. "No. At home."

"Got a job?"

"I'm in school," he repeated.

Spike stopped her scrubbing and shot him a look of utter contempt. "So you spend all day studying something you can do perfectly well already, and you don't generate any income. What're you planning to do once the gravy train is tapped out?"

Lee's first thought was that Spike was misusing the "gravy train" expression. Malaprops, spoonerisms—Lee picked them out of conversations every day. There was something disconcerting about Spike's surety, though, and before he could ask what she meant, Roman hopped back into the small clearing, mostly dressed, pulling on a pointy black boot. "Thanks for being so gracious to my guest."

Spike huffed, never taking her eyes from her beads.

"C'mon, Lee." Roman herded him out the door. "Not all Tax Rats are raging assholes. I promise." With Lee following, Roman strode into the street. He set a quick pace, as if he was eager to put as much distance between them and the apartment as Lee was. "So," he said briskly. "Language."

"Language," Lee murmured. And that was all. Yesterday, if anyone had shown an interest in his studies, Lee would have been bursting with things to say. For instance, take the expression Tax Rat. Most people thought it was because there were rats in the old Taxable District buildings, and the residents lived among them. But it was worse than that. During the time of the Black Death, rats carried the fleas that carried the original bubonic plague. So Tax Rat actually meant they were filthy plague-carriers.

Not that he thought he'd score any points by trumpeting out that particular etymology in the District, whether he would ever dream of using the phrase himself or not.

Lee was about to step off a curb when Roman tugged him back. An old man on a tricycle rolled by, startlingly fast. "I really want to salvage this morning," Roman said quietly. "Because Troy and Spike don't know you like I know you. You're more than just a pretty face. I want our date to end on a good note...and not just for me."

Lee didn't know what to say—after ten years of studying words and phrases. He nodded.

They crossed the street to a cafe in an old brick building. If the Cat and Canary seemed overdecorated, the Sugar Bowl was an explosion of texture and pattern. Worn barrels bursting with flowers flanked the door. A string of bells tinkled as Roman opened the door for Lee with a flourish. Inside, the furniture was brightly painted, and no two chairs were alike. Blown glass baubles hung in the windows caught rays of sunlight slanting between the tall buildings, casting fairy-like dots of light and color on the walls. It was magical, in a weird way, once you got past the fact that the paint was probably the only thing holding everything together.

Emma would have been fascinated, but Lee had never allowed his sister to tempt him so far into the District. He must have sensed they weren't really welcome. And, he was now realizing, maybe Mr. Babcock wasn't naturally grim after all—maybe he was sick of his shop being so close to the highway, and having to deal with all the ignorant Boomers wandering through.

They seated themselves at a wobbly table by the window. A cup of crayon stubs sat on each tabletop beside the ketchup and mustard, and the walls were covered in doodles, some awkward, some obscene, and some beautiful. Each of the hand-printed menus was decorated with colored stickers, all suns and raindrops. Studying the ubiquitous District stickers very nearly distracted Lee from the alarming prices. "You don't have to treat," he said. "It's too much. I'll pay for my own."

"You think I can't afford breakfast?"

"I didn't say that. It's the prices. They're all...."

"Lee." Roman's hand fell to Lee's wrist. "Look at me. Don't worry about the prices."

But how could he not? While his needs were provided for by his family and he enjoyed the luxury of really exploring his field of research, Roman worked multiple jobs with nothing to show for it but a closet.

Lee scrambled to find the cheapest thing on the menu as the waitress filled Roman's coffee cup, then turned Lee's over and did the same. Roman sat back and chatted briefly with her. The waitress smiled at Lee. He smiled back, dreading the moment her opinion of him would be ruined by his accent.

"I'll have the regular," Roman said.

"Four-egg omelet and a half-stack, extra syrup. Got it. And for you?"

Lee did his best not to "hammer" his plosives. "Toast."

The waitress waited for the rest of his order. When he finished with an apologetic shrug, she scrunched her face in puzzlement.

"That's all," Lee said. Then he added, "Revenge of the Orange Malt."

The waitress shook her head in sympathy, jotted down the order and headed toward the kitchen.

Once she was gone, Roman gazed at Lee for a long

moment, head cocked, a small, saddish smile on his face. Then he leaned forward on his elbows and murmured, "You didn't drink *that* much."

"It's fine. I'm not a big breakfast-eater."

"I can't get you off. I can't feed you. Kinda makes me wonder..." Roman spread his arms to indicate himself. "What's in it for you?"

"Plenty."

"Yeah?" Roman quirked an eyebrow skeptically. "Your family's got enough drama going on, what with the wedding, and here you are staying out all night. You sure it's worth the grief?"

"It's worth it."

Roman rested his chin on his fist and gazed up into the opalescent glass bauble hanging over their table. "We'll see."

The waitress returned with their food, and Lee's mouth watered at the sight of Roman's full plate. In the center of the small plate in front of him, his own pitiful slice of toast just looked sad. He took small bites and interspersed them with sips of coffee to make them last, and even so, he finished well before Roman.

"More toast?" Roman said. "I can flag down the waitress."

"No, no thanks. I'm...full." Lee hoped his stomach didn't punctuate his statement with an empty growl.

"Food's safe to eat here, y'know. District shops get inspected out the yin-yang."

"I didn't mean to imply.... I didn't think it was contaminated. Honest."

Roman eyed him. "Okay. So what's really bugging you?"

"Nothing." Lee forced himself to meet Roman's shrewd gaze. "I had a great time."

"Huh. Just imagine how impressed you'd be if you actually shot your load."

The waitress saved Lee from fumbling for a reply by checking back to see if they needed a refill on their coffee. "No thanks," Roman said, with a hint of resignation. "We'll settle up now. Martinville filters?"

"Small or large?"

"Large."

She glanced down at her notepad and did a quick calculation. "Three."

"Three? Highway robbery."

The waitress considered. "I'll throw in a muffin to go, but that's the best I can do."

Roman sighed dramatically. "Fine." Goods changed hands. Roman dug three sealed water filters out of his leather jacket and handed them over. The waitress brought him a bran muffin that he offered to split with Lee.

Lee very nearly accepted. But he was so baffled about Roman paying for their breakfast with water filters, he could only shake his head. Roman shrugged and crammed the muffin into his pocket.

The early morning sun slanted into Lee's eyes as they emerged from the cafe, and Roman pointed out the direction of a recognizable street and detailed which landmarks would lead back to Cat and Canary. Despite the early hour, Lee knew it was late enough that once he got home, he'd have some explaining to do.

Roman gave him a parting hug—a press of bodies accompanied by a provocative grind that was over far too soon—and said, "What a shame. I hoped you'd be different."

Different from all the other Benefit Boomers, or

different from the way he actually was? "How?"

"You didn't trust me...with breakfast, I mean."

"I hadn't realized it was a test."

"I can handle your ignorance. But your pity? That's a lot tougher to digest."

Before Lee could answer, Roman had spun on his heel, striding back into the depths of the Tax District, all long legs and swagger.

Lee swallowed around the sour coffee aftertaste. Last night, in that fleeting, pre-sleep moment with Roman cradled against his side, Orange Malt and semen on his tongue and the scent of woodsmoke in his nostrils, he felt as if he'd peeled off a protective barrier and experienced the world anew. Now, though, that rawness only intensified the sting of seeing Roman walk away.

9

If Mr. Babcock hadn't been outside Cat and Canary washing his windows, Lee would have simply used the store as a familiar landmark, one that informed him he was on the border of the Benefit Sector, that much closer to a shuttle home. But the old man was there with a bucket full of sudsy water and a long-handled brush, scrubbing the big pane of glass. And although Lee could have slunk past without Babcock noticing, he felt that failing to acknowledge the shopkeeper would simply prove that Boomers were as overprivileged and oblivious as everyone in the District thought.

"Happiness and hope, Mr. Babcock."

Babcock looked over his shoulder, frowned in recognition, and turned back to the soapy window. "Shop's closed. We open at noon."

"Yes. I know." He'd been coming to Cat and Canary for years. He was well aware of the hours. "Just being polite."

Lee kept walking, but from the corner of his eye, in the window he saw Babcock do a double-take at his reflection. "Isn't that the shirt I sold you?" he called out.

Lee paused, recalling the transaction in an entirely

new light. It was the shirt he'd been offered in exchange for the Boomer magazine he'd been reading. At the time, he found it bizarre on many levels—not only being offered clothing at a bookstore, but trading a magazine for it he was going to recycle anyway. Lee turned to face Babcock and said, "Not exactly. We bartered." Babcock narrowed his eyes in appraisal. "All these years. You could have just said something if you didn't want me to pay cash."

"Took you long enough to figure it out." The old man turned back to his window. The flip side of the long-handled scrub brush had a squeegee attached. He put all his attention into stripping gray water off the window, even though the reflection clearly showed Lee expecting him to participate in a conversation. When Lee didn't give up and go away, Babcock stopped squeegeeing with a roll of his eyes. "So what more do you want from me?"

"Tell me what I'm supposed to pay you with. Water filters? Sugar?"

Babcock spat out a laugh, possibly the first one Lee had ever elicited from him. "Do I look like a moonshiner?"

"I have no idea."

Babcock tilted back his head and gave the air a sniff. "You smell like smoke. So that's where you've been. You didn't show up early—you're doing the walk of shame." He laughed again, more bitterly now. "Hope she was worth it. Your wife will have a few choice words for you when you show your face back home."

"I'm not married," Lee said coldly, "I'm still in school. Plus, it's not a she, it's a he."

"Queer, huh?" Babcock didn't seem particularly shocked. "I'd be less vocal about that if I were you. It's one thing to make that kind of announcement here in the District, but be careful who you brag to back home, where your family is counting on your wedding to keep 'em exempt. Not that you've got any reason to listen to an old fart like me, who won't even tell you what he barters."

He'd turned back to his damn window again. Ten years of patronage meant so little to him? Fine. So be it. Lee was just about to stride off in disgust when he realized Babcock was tapping at a spot on the window where cutesy plastic clings were stuck inside. Wheels. Circles. Suns. Decorated like the cafe menu with its sun and rain stickers.

No rain drops here, so...no water filters.

He had no idea what the sun or circles might mean, but he'd seen the wheels before, last night at the bonfire. And there'd been shuttle tokens in the bucket. Cat and Canary was right off the highway, which meant he'd probably do well bartering... "Shuttle tokens."

Babcock plunged his brush into the soapy water and sloshed it up and down with a vengeance. "So. Maybe you're not that slow after all."

* * *

The ride back to the Benefit Sector went by faster than usual. The shuttle made all its typical stops, and although Lee was seeing everything through new eyes, the roads hadn't magically grown shorter. He was simply lost in thought. He'd glimpsed another world, a world where money was devalued and symbols replaced numbers. It had been there all along, and he'd never noticed.

The secret barter system wasn't distressing—not

when he wasn't trying to trade something ridiculous, anyhow—but he wondered what other mysterious dealings had been happening right under his nose. He was so preoccupied as he disembarked and strode across the platform, it took him a moment to realize the ticket taker was chasing after him. It struck him as odd, since the time to check tickets was before someone got on, not after they got off. And doubly odd, since she was calling him by name.

He was about to show his receipt, but paused with his hand on his wallet. The ticket taker jogged after him, red-faced and winded. "Are you Lee?" she gasped.

Briefly, he considered denying it. But why bother? He had proof of payment.

"I am."

"I got a message for you from your sister." Her diction wasn't as crisp as Lee's, but it was still a Boomer accent, only less educated. Poorer. "She says she covered for you. She says go inside the back door and right to your room."

"But, why?"

"She didn't say." The ticket taker assessed Lee, then added, "But she said the info would be worth a fiver to ya."

Unlikely, since Emma didn't use that sort of slang. But luckily Lee did have an emergency five-dollar bill folded small behind a picture in his wallet. And luckily he still had his wallet, too.

As he approached his house from the alley and slipped in to the sound of raised voices, he considered what it was, exactly, that Emma thought she'd "covered." For all anyone knew—anyone other than Roman's housemates—the only reason he'd braved the Bonfires was for the music.

It felt childish to lie about where he'd been. But unless he told everyone about Roman, whatever he said about his District adventures would be nothing more than a half-truth anyway. Tensions were high enough over the wedding, so it was best not to talk about it right this very minute. He slipped into the house, stripped off his smoky clothes and ducked into the bathroom for as long a shower as he dared take without setting off the water conservation alerts and giving Mom something more to worry about.

As he shuffled from the bathroom to his bedroom with a towel around his waist, Mom called out, "So, you're finally up. Glad you could join us."

Emma rushed out of her room and squeezed past him in the hallway with her wedding dress over one shoulder and a shoebox cradled to her chest. "You're hungover," she whispered. "I told them to let you sleep."

The protective plastic around the dress shushed him as she bustled away—to go get ready to marry Howard. "Emma, wait," he whispered urgently.

She spun around in a huge rustle of plastic and tulle, eyebrows raised. "What now?"

"Did you ever think about...calling off the wedding?"

"And then what? Live with Mom and Dad for the rest of my life? I don't think so. That's your tactic, Lee. Not mine."

10

LEE LOOKED AT THE event hall as if he was seeing it for the very first time. Suddenly everything felt surreal, from the balloons to the ice sculpture—and, no, he couldn't tell where Roman had chipped off a piece. He'd seen most of his extended family just a few months ago at his cousin Carl's wedding, yet they all looked different to him now, pale and tidy and manicured. No spikes. No facial piercings. No neck tattoos.

He sat dutifully beside his mother in the front row as his sister signed the marriage license, even though each stroke of the pen cut his heart like a knife. And then the Officiant Notary came forward, a stout older woman with an imposing air. She slipped on her reading glasses and analyzed the documents while a guitarist twiddled through some bland classical piece. Had the Reading of the Reports taken this long at Carl's ceremony? It seemed to go on forever. Lee glanced at Mom. She was leaning slightly forward in her chair. Her eyelashes glittered with tears. Beside her, Dad looked slightly baffled, though that was nothing new. They thought everything was normal. Just wait until the Notary discovered some irregularity, though—a distant link between the two families, or a history of birth defect the Algorithm had somehow missed, or the fact that Howard was descended from a long line of jerks—any reason at all why Emma should not be joined to him in matrimony. Then they'd all see that Lee was absolutely right to avoid putting the entire family through a similar ordeal.

Just as Lee reached for Mom's hand in hopes of softening the blow, the Notary took up the majestic white plume, dipped it in the inkwell that would only be used once, on this particular day, and penned her elaborate signature. The crowd sighed and murmured. She turned to the audience, slipped off her reading glasses with a flourish, and said, "By the power vested in me by Zone Twelve and the Bureau of Deeds and Records, I now pronounce you husband and wife. Howard, Emma, you may now kiss."

Lee thought he'd never bring himself to watch, but it turned out that he couldn't tear his eyes away. Emma closed her eyes, and Howard did, too. They didn't press up against one another, not like Lee had with Roman, but there were yards of tulle and a massive bouquet between them. And although there was no groping, no tongues, it still felt wrong that such an intimate display would happen in public.

The kiss was over in less than a second, but in that fleeting moment, years of suppressed emotions flooded through Lee. Mourning over the loss of the relationship he'd shared with Emma mingled with the sadness that things would never be the same. But mostly distress over the knowledge that he couldn't possibly bring himself to do what Emma had just done, to allow a nameless, faceless, soulless Algorithm to select a match for him that he could never love.

Emma turned to face the cheering audience. If she was crying, Lee knew, he'd never be able to contain himself. But, no. Emma was smiling. Not in happiness, not exactly. More like a triumphant display of determination, and possibly relief.

He wasn't close enough to Emma in the reception line to speak with to her, and maybe that was for the best, since he had no idea what to say. His whole body felt numb. He went through the motions, shaking hands, thanking guests, and occasionally glancing across at Howard's younger sister, who looked even more bored and vacant than she had at the rehearsal dinner.

It wasn't until the clatter of a dropped chafing dish startled him that Lee realized he'd soon have more pressing matters on his mind. He gave his third cousin a distracted handshake while searching for that familiar black silhouette. Nearly all the men were in black—it was a formal occasion, after all—but no one else carried himself like Roman, with that all-shoulders gait, striding purposefully as if to lead a charge into enemy territory.

Lee continued to cycle through the empty greetings, *Happiness and hope—thanks for coming—me? Not yet, I'm still in school.* And by the time he'd repeated the words so many times they no longer sounded like words, by the time he'd spotted several other servers many times over, Roman was still nowhere to be seen. Eventually, when all the guests had been greeted and people began to find their seats, Lee slipped away from his family and made his way toward the kitchen.

Now that it was full of food trays and caterers, it looked nothing like the dim stainless steel warren in which he'd first pressed his lips to Roman's. The workers all looked up, only curious at first, until some-one muttered, "That's the brother," and they all began working more briskly.

Lee wanted to tell them to just act like he wasn't there, but that would be useless. He was a Boomer, after all. And at least for tonight, they were employed by his family. So was Roman. If Lee felt awkward before, now that he realized how the workers perceived him, he was mortified. He turned on his heel and slunk back to his place at the main table. He wasn't sure what he'd wanted to say anyhow. Just that he wanted so badly to see the man he'd spent the night with, to reassure himself the encounter had actually happened, it was impossible to think of anything else.

 Once the guests made their way to their tables and the salads were served, Lee finally spotted Roman at a table where Mom's boss and his wife sat with their neighbors and some college friends of Dad's. Roman didn't see Lee. Of course he didn't. He was busy making sure he didn't drop croutons on anybody.

The teenager across from Lee gave a belabored sigh, and began meticulously separating carrot shreds from the lettuce. Lee didn't mean to stare, but since Roman was no longer circulating through the room, there was nothing better to look at. The girl—his *sister-in-law*—took his observation for interest, and announced, "I'm so sick of weddings."

A simple enough statement, but it had Lee puzzled. Just as no one had ever told him they wanted fewer vacation days, or less dessert, no one had ever told him they were sick of weddings. "How come?"

"What do you care?"

Lee shrugged. "Just curious."

"They're all the same. Poofy white dress. Lame

wedding band. Ugly rental hall. Stringy broiled chicken. And the Notary getting wasted on the open bar. It's the bride's day, that's what they all say, so why should I have to dress up like I think I'm some fairy princess? Mom says I should support some new local talent, but I think I'd rather design my own gown. And my colors will be red and black. Or silver and black. Or no, wait, transparent and black, and I can have stripes of clear vinyl running through the fabric. Yeah. That'd be totally cool. And my father can keep his raw squab—and his business partners too. That's what it's all about for him. Looking to impress those stuffed shirts by doing everything traditional. But not me. I'd serve nothing but sturgeon roe and pale champagne decorated with clouds of squid ink, and sign our license at midnight."

Lee had never once imagined a single detail from his own wedding. Maybe, at one time, he would have presumed it was because weddings were the bride's day and he was the groom. Now, though....

"So, why aren't you married yet?" the girl asked.

The answer came easily—he'd given it so many times that night, he lost count. "I'm still in school."

"Why? Did you fail a bunch of grades?"

"No, nothing like that. I'm studying language, and it's complicated. Subtle. It would be a shame to cram it all into a few years."

"If you say so." The girl scraped away as much dressing as she could, ate a single lettuce wedge, then abandoned the salad entirely.

Servers streamed out from the kitchen to clear the salad course and begin serving the ubiquitous banquet chicken, which undoubtedly *would* be stringy. Lee caught another glimpse of Roman placing an entree on the table while the guests paid him as much attention as they might a piece of furniture. How could they possibly fail to notice him? To Lee's eyes, it was as if everyone else in the room looked vague and muted, while Roman was strikingly clear.

While his sister-in-law weighed the merits of black dahlias versus black lilies, Lee watched Roman maneuvering through the crowd, cool and calm, intriguingly alert. If he hoped to skirt around his awkward behavior in the cafe (let alone his awkward behavior in bed) he now realized it was useless to try and gloss anything over. Roman saw everything. Probably more clearly than Lee did, himself.

While most of him wanted to crawl away and die, a more insistent part yearned for Roman so strongly, it was impossible to stop staring. Being known in the stark nakedness of his reality would be excruciating. But letting Roman slip through his fingers was unthinkable.

Lee watched the servers cycle through the tables, noting the pattern of their clearing and serving. There would be a lull in which the guests could work on their entrees. No one was in a hurry, since the longer people filled time eating dinner, the less they'd ultimately drink. During that lull, Lee excused himself. If anyone noticed him heading for a restroom that was illogically far from his table, no one mentioned it. And it put him in just the right position to find Roman on his way to clearing the tables. Lee plucked at his sleeve and lured him into a dim hallway, only then realizing he was unsure what to say. "Hi."

Roman paused for an uncomfortably long moment, then said, "Hi."

"I tried to find you earlier. I wanted to...I thought we'd have more of a chance to talk." Not only were words failing him, but Lee had no idea what to do with his hands, either.

He caught Roman's wrist, but only for a moment, before Roman pulled away and glanced toward the kitchen door, where servers were still filing out. "Probably not the best place."

"You're working," Lee said. "I know. I'm sorry."

Roman cocked his head. "I'm not the one who needs to worry. My worst-case scenario is that the boss chews me out for slacking off. I'm talking about you." If it was a violation of etiquette to leave the table, Lee was unaware of it. He was about to say so when Roman leaned in and murmured, "Do you really want your entire social circle to see you putting the make on a Tax Rat—another *guy*, no less? Your school excuse is wearing thin enough as it is. Best not push it."

Lee didn't know which was worse, the ugly slur, or the idea that anything sexual would be insinuated based on the fact that they were talking together. Either way, he wasn't about to let Roman slip away without a fight. Roman attempted to veer around him and escape into the stream of waitstaff, but Lee backed him into the wall. "Look—after tonight, who knows when I'll see you again? I should've just listened to you at the diner and let you buy me breakfast, and I'm sorry. I came off like a stuck-up Boomer. But only because I cared so much about what you thought of me."

Roman gave Lee long, assessing look, and maybe, just maybe, a ghost of a smile. Hopefully that's what it was, and not a trick of the lighting and a heaping helping of wishful thinking.

"Give me another chance," Lee said.

A few feet away, the bathroom door opened. Lee's great uncle tottered out, a venerable, leathery man who'd outlived his father's aunt by two decades. He gave Lee a myopic nod, fumbling with his fly. Roman straightened and said to Lee, "Certainly, sir, I'll see to table twelve right away."

The old man wandered by as if Roman was invisible. When he was gone, they both let out a breath. "Was that really necessary?" Lee muttered.

"Bulletproof, or naive. I can't quite decide." Either way, it seemed a step up from pitying and ignorant.

A pair of servers emerged from the kitchen laughing. They did a double-take at Lee and quelled the laughter immediately. Lee barely restrained himself from rolling his eyes. "Please," he said softly. "Let's try again."

"As much as I'd relish the chance to give you a more satisfying repeat performance, I'm thinking that's not the best idea." Before Lee could attempt to persuade him otherwise, Roman slipped off to a table where second cousins made polite conversation with Dad's coworkers, and began to clear away plates of half-eaten chicken.

Lee got back to his own table just as the server was taking away his untouched plate. Just as well. He was so crushed, he couldn't have forced anything down if he tried. His sister-in-law watched with a slightly curled lip. When the server turned to go, she said, "And I'd hire good-looking local waiters for my wedding. Not these scuzzy District thugs."

She was only a dumb teenager—and still, Lee hoped the server hadn't heard. Despite the fact that he hadn't been the one to voice the opinion, he was still sitting at the same table with this obnoxious little twit. Not serving her.

"Or I could just stay in school," she said, "like you. That would show my dad a thing or two."

Lee was so busy trying to pick Roman out from a cluster of waiters near the kitchen, he almost let the remark slip past. But something about her inflection snagged his attention. "What's that supposed to mean?"

"You're thirty, aren't you?" She gave Lee a look so filled with "duh" she might as well have shouted the word over the listless cover song the wedding band was wrapping up. "That's when tuition kicks in."

"Lee." Mom stood behind him now, shaking him by the shoulder. "It's time."

He tore himself from his plans and looked up at her, blinking. Time for what?

Oh no. The speech.

11

FROM THE STAGE, THE banquet hall looked nothing at all
like it had the morning before. Then again, Lee could
say the same for pretty much everything. Those weird
little stickers were a secret code. The District residents
despised him for merely existing. And the people he
was supposed to fit in with were insufferable.

Filled with dread that was increasing by the second,
Lee approached the microphone. He'd practiced nothing. Written nothing. He'd spend years studying language, and here he was, at the most important occasion
in Emma's life, at a loss for words.

*People want to get a look at the spouse so they can gossip
later, and they wanna get plowed. Get your new brother-in-
law's name right and you can say just about anything.*

Right.

"Happiness and hope," Lee began, and before he
could welcome the guests and thank them for coming—
and prove that he damn well knew Howard's name—it
occurred to him that maybe *how are you* would have
been more appropriate for the occasion. Because
happiness was phenomenally subjective. The status
quo was popular for a reason: most people wanted a

traditional wedding with a white gown, an inoffensive band, banquet chicken and an open bar. And maybe some people did want squid ink in their champagne. Lee might have thought it was all simply a ploy for attention, but it would be hypocritical to think that he knew what was better for someone else. After all, for some people, for him, happiness meant not marrying at all.

"Of course, I wish you all happiness and hope. What kind of monster would I be if I didn't?" Nervous laughter rippled through the crowd. "But have you ever thought about why we say it? People used to simply greet each other with *hello*—and out in the rural districts, some still do. And the etymology is actually somewhat disturbing. Hello is an alteration of the word *holla*, which means stop, cease. Blunt, maybe, but sweet and to the point, and not problematic in itself. Except that *holla* was mainly used to hail a ferryman." And after the antibiotic-immune strain of *yersinia pestis* swept the world, well, hailing the ferryman was something people tended to avoid.

Lee glanced up. Most of the facial expressions he could identify looked befuddled. He assured himself it meant his family and friends were interested in what he had to say.

"*Happiness and hope* was actually the Purity Party's final campaign slogan, before the party system was disbanded altogether so the government could focus its resources on providing health care and rebuilding the population. Maybe people don't think much about politics anymore, but the legacy remains. Happiness and hope."

Lee had been taught that it was best to pick out one person at a time when lecturing and focus on them.

He saw his neighbor from across the street, a young mother who'd always been friendly. Her mouth was slightly open, her brows twisted together. He shifted his focus to his uncle, who frowned.

"What is happiness, really? When we wish one another happiness, do we want them to have rewarding work? Or an engaging hobby? Or a compatible spouse? Many of us don't really know. The word *happiness* is so subjective, it's rare that when we offer it up in greeting, we're thinking of anything specific, or really, anything at all. The meaning is lost. The sentiment is empty."

The hairs on the back of Lee's neck prickled, and he could no longer deny that *everyone* in the room was staring at him in a mute, dumbfounded confusion. All but one, a lanky server in black who was leaning on the far wall, head cocked, arms crossed, elbows jutting to either side, and his shrewd eyes fixed on Lee.

Well. At least someone understands me.

Lee was unable to look away, and words failed him. Roman shook his head slowly and smiled a melancholy smile. Maybe the real trouble with happiness was that it was so elusive. But before he could say so and plunge the wedding guests deeper into confusion, Roman made a drinking gesture that pulled him from his introspection enough to try and wrap things up.

Lee turned to address his sister directly. "Emma, it's not for me to dictate what will make you happy. I hope you have exactly the life you want, whether that involves a new composite house in the Benefit Sector with Howard where you have a boy and a girl and a nine-to-five-job with good benefits, or...anything else your heart desires. I wish you every happiness, and should you ever be faced with hardship, a deep and abiding hope."

The guests gave a collective sigh of relief and tipped back their champagne flutes. As Lee made his way back to his seat, he noticed that Howard's father seemed annoyed, and Mom was looking at him strangely. Emma caught his sleeve and murmured, "You're such a character. I'll miss sharing a wall with you."

"I'll bet no one thought they'd be getting an education," Howard said. Not dismissively, either. He'd settled his hand atop Emma's, and he actually did look happy enough. Maybe he wouldn't turn out to be so bad after all. Lee could always hope.

* * *

For once, Lee noticed, his knees weren't up around his ears in the cramped backseat. It should have felt luxurious to spread himself out. It didn't. His hand dropped to the cushion. Normally it would brush up against Emma's. Now there was nothing there to touch, just an empty space.

Lee's stomach churned from too little food and too much vodka. Dad was busy seeing if he could name all the songs the wedding band had covered while Mom focused on driving. Even after they locked on to the highway, she fixed her eyes on the road and said nothing.

It was late by the time they got home. Lee supposed it had been a long day for everyone, though for him it felt like an entire lifetime of revelations had occurred. And yet, he wasn't tired, he was beyond tired. Numb. But not really. Although his environment felt as if it had been muffled, muted or swaddled, the dull ache in his gut permeated everything.

He'd need to pick through his transcript and

calculate exactly how many credits he had, and go over his courses to see if there was enough time to fail any of them. The notion of letting a semester of hard work go to waste didn't appeal to him, but the thought of standing up in front of his family and kissing some poor faceless woman was downright distressing.

Sleep eluded him. It was a few hours before dawn when he crept from his room to scour the recycling. Hopefully, he'd find a copy of last semester's catalog to get a better idea of the cost of tuition and ramifications of dropping to part time. The house was so quiet, so utterly still, that he let out a yelp when he rounded the corner and found Mom sitting in the living room.

"Oh, for heaven's sake, Lee," she loud-whispered. "You nearly gave me a heart attack."

"Sorry." So much for rummaging through the recycling. Unless he wanted to answer a bunch of questions about it, he'd be better off waiting until both his parents were at work. Instead he pretended he'd been heading for the kitchen. "Dehydrated."

He drank a glass of water, discovered he actually was pretty dry, and filled another to take to his room. But the clean getaway he envisioned was not to be. Mom patted the couch cushion. Lee stepped around the squares of fabric laid out on the floor in front of her and dutifully sat. Mom said, "The sheer amount of drinking you've been doing lately—this had better not be a trend."

"It's just the wedding...everything going on...don't worry, I'm not turning into an alcoholic."

"We've all been under a lot of strain." Mom leaned forward and switched a blue square with slightly different blue square. Fabric that the pickers in the District had supposedly salvaged, though it was more likely someone had only made it look that way with sandpaper and bleach water. Lee squinted to see if he could visualize the final pattern all sewn and quilted together, but he couldn't. At this early stage, without the intricate hand-stitched seams and lines, the fabric squares didn't look like much of anything. Just material. Blues. Creams. A bit of brown....

Lee choked on his water as all the implications of what he was seeing began to unspool. Wedding colors—not Emma's, but *his*. Mom watched him cough, frowning. He sputtered, got his breathing back under control, then pointed to a cream-and-blue square in the corner. "Up there...was that the shirt I wore in first grade?"

"Which shirt?"

The cream shirt with the blue checks, obviously. "For the class picture."

Mom turned her frown to the corner of the quilt, studied it for a moment, then said, "Huh. I guess it did look something like that, but no, that shirt isn't anything I've been saving. Lee..." she caught his wrist and stroked it with her thumb. "This isn't for you. It's a baby quilt."

"Oh."

"Emma wants to start her family right away."

"Oh," he repeated stupidly. He supposed it was better than adding, *And get it over with.*

Mom switched the blue squares back the way they were. "Is there something you want to tell me?"

Like what? Like he'd kissed one the caterers, an intense, smart, unflappable man named Roman? That he'd gone to the Bonfires, *alone*, then spent the night in the District—in Roman's bed—and now he was questioning everything? Lee shifted uncomfortably. "Not really."

Mom stared at the quilt for a long moment, then nodded.

12

In the end, it wasn't math that would be Lee's undoing, but law. He tried to educate himself on taxes at the campus library, but he felt too exposed, as if any moment someone would leap out and demand his thesis. In the end, he'd slunk away to a place where he felt safe—paradoxically so, since it was at the edge of the District, where exit-ramp fender benders occurred with disturbing frequency, and people got pickpocketed despite the fact that their money was practically worthless. Hopefully Cat and Canary offered more than just predictable thrillers and vintage cookbooks full of hilarious casseroles.

When Lee asked for a book pertaining to remedial business math, Old Babcock gave him a slim volume on tax penalties instead. Lee figured he was expected to pay for the book. He slid a shuttle token across the counter. Babcock made a "keep going" gesture and Lee paid another. Babcock accepted with a nod and a grunt. As Lee headed toward one of the many cluttered nooks where he and Emma used to pore through strange old tomes together, Babcock said aloud, as if to himself, "People who don't haggle might come off like a sucker.

No one respects a sucker."

Because the District residents need yet another reason to loathe me.

Lee ignored the sinking feeling in his stomach and eased down onto the floor with his purchase. He hadn't minded paying two tokens. It wasn't just the book that had been bartered for, but the privacy in which to study it—though with his flimsy grasp on numbers, Lee didn't hold out much hope for the faded paperback. Not until he realized that the information inside was exactly what he wanted to know.

The tables and figures confounded him, but no wonder. The true cost of anything was as cryptic as a list price on a District menu. Things like food and shelter and vehicles had costs, but these figures were either mitigated by subsidies or multiplied by taxes. The red tape around education was particularly thick. One thing society valued was a well-educated population...at least in theory. Lee had always thought public school was free, but he hadn't considered that the money to pay for infrastructure and staff must come from somewhere. Those expenses were subsidized by taxes. Unlike primary education, higher education was only subsidized for Benefit Boomers. Specifically, Boomers under the age of thirty. After that, the full brunt of the tuition was the family's responsibility. So *that* was what his sister-in-law's remark meant. The family that would soon start losing its other exemptions once he graduated and didn't marry.

Lee emerged from the dusty niche between the shelves with a good theoretical sense of what was going on, but no concrete idea what to do about it. No other customers were in the store. Babcock was seated behind the register reading a newspaper. Without looking up—in fact, without even a pause in his reading—he asked, "Find what you were looking for?"

"Mostly." What he couldn't quite grasp was how all these contingencies would affect him. "How much do you suppose the mortgage would run on a small composite house?"

Babcock allowed the corner of his paper to droop. He met Lee's eye and raised an eyebrow. "Do I look like I know squat about composite houses? I live upstairs. Brick and wood."

It didn't matter. If Lee payed attention, he could probably find a mortgage statement in the recycling. But his parents would wonder why he was asking if he tried to determine the family's current income. "And how much do you think a technician at a water plant would make? Or a municipal clerk?"

Babcock didn't answer, just continued thumbing through his paper. Lee thought he was being dismissed because his question was too ignorant to even warrant a response, but then the old man teased out a sheet and shoved it across the counter. "Check the want ads and see."

Lee hadn't looked at the want ads since the high school summer he spent cleaning offices for minimum wage...a job which, he now saw, had been subsidized to allow it to be performed by a Boomer. He picked through the ads, and while he didn't see the exact positions his parents held, and while he'd have to account for things like seniority and expertise, the bottom line was clear enough.

If Lee didn't figure out something soon, his family was screwed.

* * *

Landing a job interview on campus was easy. Lee had always been an eager student, and each of his advisors was happy to furnish him with a glowing recommendation. Within a week, the head of the Language Arts Department had agreed to meet with him. Although Lee had never officially studied under the man, the two of them had chatted at enough academic functions over the years that they were on a first-name basis.

"I'm sorry to say there isn't a tenured position available at the moment," George told him, "but don't be put off by the adjunct title. Several tenured faculty have hinted that they're looking at retirement within the next couple of years."

"My main concern is the tuition discount." The *massive* discount he'd discovered that reduced tuition to a mere token payment. "It still applies to adjunct faculty. Right?"

"Absolutely, anyone who teaches at least two classes. If you're willing to put in the work, the University's thrilled to help you bolster your credentials." Lee's heart pounded. He hadn't realized how much he actually wanted a PhD, how satisfying it would be to stop spreading out his work and actually sink his teeth into the subject matter. George scanned his transcripts for the third time. "With grades like these—and the depth and breadth of your coursework—you're certainly qualified to teach any of our 100- and 200-level courses, and we'd be lucky to have you. Not exactly riveting subject matter, but not a bad paycheck for someone just starting out."

Probably not, if he was looking to start a family. But his main goal was to give himself some space to figure out what to do about the Algorithm without burdening his parents with the loss of their exemptions. If he was still taking at least nine credits in a degree-seeking program, which he would be, then his family would retain its current status. He was sure of it; he'd studied that section of the tax code until he could recite it in his sleep.

Lee had a plan. Teaching two classes and taking three more would be the bare minimum to make it fly, and he'd be busy, very busy. But if that's what he needed to do, he'd gladly do it.

After all, Roman was busy working multiple jobs. It wasn't as if he had a bunch of free time to spare.

And there was the crux of it all, the fleeting prize that Lee had barely allowed himself to admit he coveted. Racking up more degrees was really just an excuse. What he truly yearned for was Roman. Hard to say whether Roman wanted to spend more time with him, or whether they'd only had the elusive "hookup" Lee read about once in a crumbling paperback that seemed to be primarily about drinking mimosas and buying shoes. Either way, a good job and the freedom to stay in school would give him the opportunity to find out.

"So tell me, Lee." George scanned the transcripts again. "How's the thesis coming—what was it, something to do with phrases that have fallen out of usage?"

"You know how research can expand to take up as much time as you're willing to give it. But now it's just a matter of putting it on paper." Lee was certain. Now that he was motivated, he could probably get it all down in a weekend.

"I look forward to perusing it."

George wasn't required to read any further than

the advisors' synopses and comments. Lee beamed with pride.

"How are you set for housing at the moment?" George asked.

"It's not an issue. My parents have always been supportive."

"Still at home, hm? It's worth checking out the on-campus housing. If any grad student bungalows go unclaimed, new faculty can rent them for a fraction of the cost. It'll save you the commute—and I'm sure your wife will appreciate having a place to yourselves."

"It's...just me. I'm not married."

George cocked his head and looked at Lee as if he must be mistaken about his own marital status. "I could swear I saw an announcement about the Ford-Kennedy wedding a couple weeks back."

"That was my sister." And Howard. Who hadn't killed each other yet, last time Lee spoke to Emma.

George still seemed puzzled. He flipped through Lee's transcript and peered intently through his bifocals. "But you're thirty."

"Twenty-nine." For a few more months, at least.

George shifted his focus to Lee's face, eyes flicking up over the top of his glasses. It was as if, in that single glance, he suddenly saw Lee for what he was, not what everyone presumed he should be. And given the excruciating moment of stony silence that followed, George didn't care for what he saw.

Lee added, "Transitioning from student to teacher will be challenging enough." He didn't think he sounded defensive. At least, he hoped he didn't. "And being single, I'll have more energy to devote to the job."

"Of course, the final decision doesn't rest with me." Was there a coolness to George's tone that wasn't there before, or was he just imagining it? "Human resources needs to verify your transcripts and references. It may take a while, so I'd encourage you to continue your job search."

Lee's stomach sank. Only moments before, George had been acting like the adjunct professorship was a given. And now.... "The grades are from this university. And my references all teach here."

"At that point, it will be up to the Provost whether or not you move forward in the hiring process."

"Okay...."

"And, of course, the sorts of intro classes you're qualified to teach are in high demand, so it may take a few semesters to find you a spot." George tamped the stack of papers into alignment with a single severe rap. "But best of luck to you, Mr. Kennedy."

Lee shook George's hand in a daze and wondered if trying to chat with the Provost would be an exercise in futility. Given how quickly George had gone from "we'd be lucky to have you" to "Mr. Kennedy" once he'd discovered Lee wasn't yet married, anything Lee said to the Provost was unlikely to make the slightest bit of difference.

13

THE COFFEE WAS THIN and the muffin tasted like sawdust, but the cluttered District diner was the only place Lee felt like people weren't judging him for leaving the Algorithm untriggered. They did look at him strangely when he spoke—he could hardly mimic a District accent without feeling like an utter fraud—but the disapproval felt marginally less horrible when it was due only to his origins, and not his failure to live up to his duties.

During the pockets of time when class wasn't in session and his parents were at work, Lee had been on the phone with prospective employers...or, more often, their gatekeepers. Agencies, secretaries, HR departments. They all assured him they'd call back if he made it to the next stage of the process. Very few of them did.

He scanned the ads for something meaningful, or at least something interesting, but the verbiage sounded awfully familiar. Primary school language arts teacher, copy editor, publishing intern—he'd already applied for all these positions. He would have performed any of those jobs well; in fact, he was overqualified. Yet the ads were still running.

From the hundreds of calls and resumes, he'd been

offered only a handful of interviews. And of those, only two came forth with a job offer. One was from a florist who needed a deliveryman willing to haul masses of decaying plant matter to the compost site when he wasn't surprising people with bouquets, and the other was a dusty office where workers fed sheets of paper into a machine nine hours a day. Neither one required he even finish his Master's. For that matter, neither required his Bachelor's, either.

Since the pay for both jobs was about the same, it meant Lee would need to decide whether he'd rather do something nauseating, or mind-numbing. He was flipping through the ads again to see if he missed anything new when he noticed a small section he hadn't seen before, since it was wedged between Commercial Real Estate and Birth Announcements: shared rentals.

If he moved out, he'd be the only one burdened with a tax penalty, not his parents. And maybe with enough housemates....

The idea died so quickly it was practically stillborn. After taxes, Lee would need to work both the compost hauling and the paper feeder job to afford even a shared studio. At which point, he'd have fewer than six hours a day to bother sleeping in it.

He'd folded the paper on his lap and was gazing numbly at a line of ants marching down the graffiti-covered wall when the server—the same one he had before—paused to warm his coffee, and asked, "Where's your boyfriend?"

"He's not...we...." Lee dropped his menu, picked it up, then realized he was holding it upside down and slid it onto the tabletop as unobtrusively as possible. "He's at work."

Then it was the server's turn to be flustered, as the

last plosive Lee hammered rang through the diner like the clatter of a breaking saucer. She gave a tiny gasp, and then another question tumbled out in a rush. "Are you moving closer to the border so you can see more of him? That's so romantic." Was she mocking? It didn't sound like it—then again, it wouldn't be the first time Lee had no idea what was really going on. He looked her in the eye, really looked, and her cheeks went pink. "Sorry. It's none of my business."

"That's okay. Really. But rents are ridiculous, even shared. Is there a local paper where I could find something a little less...pricy?"

"Don't look in the District paper—only Boomer slumlords advertise there." She stumbled, blushing harder when she remembered she was *speaking* to a Boomer, then added, "The business cards tacked to the vestibule wall. That's what you want."

Lee finished his coffee and paid for his meal with shuttle tokens. He couldn't bring himself to haggle, but since apparently nobody tipped in the District, it was a way to leave a little something extra for the server without coming off as arrogant. After the gauntlet of discouraging strangers he'd had to navigate these past few weeks, how could he begrudge an extra few tokens to someone willing to show him a hint of kindness?

He stepped into the entryway and looked with fresh eyes. Before, he'd been dazzled by the brightly painted chairs, the sun sparkling off the glass baubles in the window and the stream of consciousness crayon journey unfolding on the walls. But now that he knew what he was seeing, he couldn't imagine how he'd missed the dozens upon dozens of business cards tacked up around the doorway. None of them said anything about rentals...though several of them were dotted with stickers. Most of the symbols he didn't know, gears and diamonds and other stylized shapes that didn't look like much of anything. But he did know one. The snowflake—sugar.

That card was creased and worn, as if it had hung there a while. It had no phone number, only a name and an address, but Lee recognized the street. Tentative plans swirled through his head as he set off to find it. He could stockpile an awful lot of sugar before he turned thirty. Enough that he wouldn't need to work two awful jobs in exchange for half a room? It seemed like a lot to hope for, but it couldn't hurt to investigate. And maybe, once he'd discovered that, between a job and a stockpile of sugar, he could afford his very own room, he'd stop by Roman's apartment on his way back to the shuttle and...maybe he wouldn't even make it back to the shuttle. Maybe he wouldn't need to.

Lee walked. He recognized more landmarks now. First the resale shop where all the clothes in the window had faded to a mismatched shade of gray. Then the gap in a row of close-packed buildings where fire had claimed something generations ago, and now a scattering of children played on monkey bars made of industrial pipe. The street was easy to find, but the address on it was farther than Lee had realized. The deeper he went into the District, the bleaker things looked.

It began with a broken window. In Roman's neighborhood, that window would have been patched—and then the patch would be painted with designs to call attention to itself. But no one cared enough about this window to board it up, let alone decorate the repair. Then an aluminum storm door, which had clearly been kicked in. It hung crookedly from its frame, as if in pain. And eventually, it wasn't just doors and windows, railings and stairs missing, but entire walls. There'd been fire here, too, but no one had built a playground in the burnt buildings. No one, in fact, had bothered finishing the demolition at all.

Lee checked the address on the business card. It led to the husk of a building. Not recently fallen, but long ago. It was possible he'd gotten the address wrong, but unlikely. Maybe he should have found a newer card. Maybe whoever hung it had moved on long ago.

It was at the moment that Lee began to suspect something wasn't quite right when someone shoved him from behind and, when he was sprawled face-down on the crumbling pavement, kicked him sharply, once, in the side of the head.

14

AMMONIA. LEE GAGGED FROM the stab to his sinuses, then turned his head and vomited.

A gray-haired woman in medical scrubs was holding the basin. Once she determined he was done heaving, she called out, "He's awake," in a thick District accent.

His vision swam. Where was he? Fluorescent lighting buzzed overhead in the narrow hallway. It was old construction, linoleum floors and plaster walls, which meant he was still in the District. He lay on a cart pushed up against the wall, and he wasn't the only one in such a condition. At his head, an old man ranted about needing his medicine, while at his feet, a young woman was quite possibly going into labor.

A man in a greenish lab coat strode up the hallway. He'd been tall once, but now he was stooped and wrinkled. Hard to tell if he was frowning or his face had just settled that way. "What's this one?" he asked. His accent was thicker than the woman's.

"Some kids found 'im over near the old box factory."

"The one out by Plymouth?"

"No...the other one, down by the Flats. Head injury, probably concussion. Came in unconscious, smelling salts brought him around. Looks like he got rolled. No wallet...but going by his shoes, he can probably afford treatment."

The man leaned over him. "Got a name, son?"

"Lee Kennedy." He did his best to quell his panic. "What time is it? How long have I been out?"

The man's eyes narrowed. "You're not from around here...are you?"

Lee tried to shake his head, but the ceiling tilted, and he began to dry-heave.

"Call the border monitor," the man in the lab coat told the woman. "The sooner we get him to a Sector hospital, the better."

"Dumbass Boomers." The woman backed away from Lee as if he had the plague. "Come down here sniffing 'round for drugs and don't even have the common sense to steer clear of the Flats."

"I wasn't looking for drugs," Lee said weakly.

But the woman probably hadn't heard. She was walking away, briskly, complaining all the while. "Taking up time and resources we need for our own. And what do we get in return? Nothing. Except maybe a fine, if we don't get him transferred quick enough for their liking."

The old man waiting in the hallway grabbed her as she passed and said, "C'mon, Sandy, I need my medicine."

"I told you to taper off, you old coot, but did you listen? We're out of morphine now, probably 'til next week. I'll get you some pills for the nausea, but that's the best I can do."

It was an agonizing wait in the dingy hallway for the Sector ambulance to show up. The woman in labor was eventually wheeled somewhere more private. The old man moaning about his medication, however, was left right where he was.

Lee wondered: had the waitress set him up to be rolled? He sorely hoped not—she'd seemed so sweet. And all those hundreds of business cards, surely not all of them were scams waiting to be triggered by ignorant Boomers out of their element. He closed his eyes and did his best to put the doubts out of his mind, without much success. He was still ruminating on the matter when the ambulance arrived.

The difference in the medical staff between the Tax District and the Benefit Sector was as pronounced as the catering waiters. Boomer medics were calm and professional, like their hospitality counterparts. And just as impersonal.

Lee's mother was waiting for him at the Sector emergency room. "What happened?" she demanded. "Are you all right?" Before Lee could answer, she turned to a medic and snapped, "Is he all right?"

"He's in good hands," the medic said blandly.

Lee imagined the nurse, Sandy, would've answered with something significantly more direct.

A neurologist soon came to conduct an examination, and Lee had to answer some simple questions and follow a pen with his eyes. The scan would take longer, though, and the wait for it felt interminable with Mom sitting there beside him, fidgeting angrily.

"I'm sorry you had to leave work," Lee said.

Mom looked at him as if she'd like to add another bruise to his head. "Don't be an ass. I don't give a damn about missing a few hours of work. Whatever this is..." she gestured vaguely at Lee. "You got off lucky. What if it had been worse? Wandering around the most dangerous part of the District—honestly, what if they'd caved that thick head of yours in?"

Lee could hardly argue when he totally agreed. He stared down at the pulse monitor clipped to his forefinger and wished a bland, impersonal nurse would wheel him off for his scan. But he supposed he'd need to go to the hospital in Emma's new neighborhood if he wanted that kind of service. And then he thought of the old man in morphine withdrawal and felt petty for even harboring the notion.

More quietly, Mom asked, "What is it you're looking for out there?"

Was she referring to the apartment hunting, or the years of sneaking off to Cat and Canary, or the night he'd spent in Roman's bed? Hard to say. That was the thing about Mom. She somehow had a knack for knowing far more than she let on.

Mom closed her eyes and sat back in resignation, and settled her hand over his, and together, they waited. Eventually Lee was carted off for scans that showed his skull was thankfully intact, given some medication to dull the pain and prevent his brain from swelling, and sent home with a caution to come back in if he experienced any further symptoms from a long and alarming list.

Mom didn't press him as to what he'd been doing in the District, but maybe it didn't matter. The main thing was, she knew.

On the doctor's recommendation, Lee stayed home the next day, and though he tried to work on his thesis, he couldn't focus. His headache was distracting, but more than that, he kept circling back to the fact that maintaining the status quo was impossible, and yet there seemed no other option. He couldn't afford tuition or housing on his own, and his family would be penalized if he stayed put and stayed single. The only way to move forward was to trigger the Algorithm and get married.

He almost wished his skull *had* been caved in. A morbid thought, to be sure, but the more he considered it, the more he realized...there must be some concessions for people who were too damaged to trigger their Algorithms.

Against medical advice, he shuttled to the campus library to embark on this new line of research, and somehow his nagging headache receded to mere background noise while his focus sharpened.

The brain was a mysterious organ. How difficult would it be to simply answer some of the neurologist's questions incorrectly? And at home, he could feign memory loss easily enough by asking when his sister would be home.

Simple, maybe. But the potential ramifications were profound. The subject of disability was fascinating. Lee would have loved to sign up for some classes next semester...if graduation hadn't become, at long last, unavoidable.

According to the texts, a disabled Benefit Boomer became a ward of the state. They'd live out their life in residential facilities where trained staff would keep them safe and entertained.

How bad would that really be?

Lee closed the book decisively. How low had he sunk, to seriously consider faking permanent brain injury as a viable alternative to marriage?

His head really did hurt, he realized, and he'd studied well into the evening. He stopped by the student health center on his way back to the shuttle to see if there was anything they could give him for the pain.

Like most residents of the Benefit Sectors, Lee was,

overall, in good health. Other than the time he nearly lost a finger to a paper cutter, he only visited the health center for the annual cheek-swab that monitored his exposure to any potentially mutated bacteria.

Staff was sparse this late at night, and the waiting room looked deserted. He rang a bell, and a nurse came out to greet him. Actually, "greet" was putting it kindly. More like she gave him a leery look and pulled on a surgical mask. She eyed him warily over the top of the fabric. "Have you experienced any of the following symptoms in the last forty-eight hours," she asked, in her clipped Boomer accent. "Shortness of breath? Nasal discharge? Nausea? Vomiting? Fever? Chills? Headache—?"

"Yes, I'm here for a headache."

The nurse's eyes went wide with alarm. "I'll need you to step into the hermetic chamber—"

"I'm not ill, I've had an injury. You can see that, can't you?" Of course she could. The bruising was quite vivid.

"It's procedure, sir. Step into the chamber and you'll be seen to shortly."

Lee was tempted to turn around and leave, but at this point, he was concerned that his leaving would trigger some sort of wellness alarm. The quarantined chamber was small and dark, a plain room the size of Roman's closet, with a minimally padded bench to sit on, and numerous sensors and gauges on the walls. At eye level, a monitor set flush in the paneling displayed the helpful hint: *Did you know...the human oral microbiome is home to over 6 billion bacteria.*

Lee folded his hands in his lap and pressed his lips firmly together.

It had been a bad idea to stop at the health center. He could have been halfway home by now, but instead he was stuck in a dim, pedantic box. While the various sensors scanned and re-scanned him to ensure he wasn't a plague-carrier, he shut his eyes and tried to figure out his next move. He might as well trigger the Algorithm. No doubt his future spouse had activated hers years ago.

His head throbbed harder. Beneath the whoosh of the filtered ventilation, the sound of distant conversation flowed as the Boomer night nurses gossiped.

"Is that a professor in there?"

"Grad student. You should see the shiner on him. Someone's husband must've shown him the door. Handsome guy like him, still single…they're always trouble."

"Better than all those pampered brats looking for speed. Hello, you don't all have ADHD. If you want to lose weight that bad, get some exercise and skip dessert."

"Or the ones who haven't figured out that booze and mid-terms don't mix."

The HEPA filter gently wheezed as the nurses moved out of range. Lee strained to hear them. A few moments later, they were back.

"What about that transfer you applied for?" one of them asked as the voices grew closer again.

"I don't know, I don't think I can go through with it."

"I thought it was a huge pay bump, and no more night shifts."

"Yes, but the taxes would be really messy. Plus, I'd be working in the District." Lee could practically hear the shudder in her voice from merely entertaining the notion. His reaction was just as visceral. Not disgust, and not fear, but a queasy, anxiety-laden excitement.

As she opened the quarantine chamber door and

light flooded in, Lee shielded his eyes. "All right, Mr. Kennedy. Scans are clear."

He stumbled out of the chamber and followed her into the treatment room, but he hardly heard her.

"I've pulled your medical records and got you authorized for an anti-inflammatory."

He nodded dumbly, having forgotten about his headache, since he was in the midst of a great epiphany. Maybe the university was unwilling to hire him if he wasn't married....

But the Taxable District had its own schools.

15

By the time Lee scored an interview at District Polytechnic Sixty-Two, his bruising had faded to a sickly yellow corona around his eye socket, flecked with cloudy patches of brownish gray. When Mom asked why he was wearing a tie, he said he was meeting with the head of the department, though he neglected to clarify that it wasn't the department in which he was currently studying. As he made his way out the front door, she caught him by the sleeve, pulled him into a brief hug, and told him, "Good luck."

He wasn't sure whether he felt unsettled, or reassured.

The District college couldn't have looked more different from the Sector university. While Lee's university was all efficient composite, pleasingly engineered to harmonize with the landscape, the Polytechnic was in a vast, rambling series of structures centuries old. Like everything in the Taxable District, it was patched over many times, with fieldstone cemented into brick, and sheet metal covering fiberglass, patch upon patch in an undulating play of texture and shape. Colors were subdued here, compared to the residential neighborhoods, where bright paint ran riot. And there were no stickers at the bursar's window. Roman had told him school wasn't cheap. Apparently, an education couldn't be funded with water filters or sugar.

If the interviews he'd had in the Sector were anything to go by, Lee expected to meet with a single person. Instead, he was greeted by a team. A young woman from human resources, a woman his parents' age who was the Provost, and much older man who was the head of Language.

It was the sort of attention Lee would expect at a second interview.

Or the sort of regard one might receive with a Boomer degree.

The HR woman introduced Lee to the group, and the Provost asked him some questions about his transcript. He'd needed to explain himself so many times, to dodge the subject of matriculating by waxing eloquent about the various avenues into which he'd focused his studies, that it was easy enough to fall into the rhythm of his academic narrative. It came so naturally, in fact, that as he spoke, the interviewers might have even forgotten about that horrible yellow-gray bruise. For a little while, at least.

"And you are on track to graduate at the end of this semester?" Professor Clark asked. It was difficult to tell if the head of the department was teasing. First, there was the accent. And then the twinkle in his eye.

Lee chose to answer as if the old man was laughing *with* him, and not *at* him. "I only need to finish my thesis." The creases around the professor's eyes deepened as his smiled, and Lee added, "If knowing that I had a teaching position waiting for me wasn't the best incentive, I don't know what could possibly top it."

"Of course you'll finish your thesis," the Provost said.

She had a brisk, no-nonsense manner about her that reminded Lee of his mother. "Even if you didn't, your transfer credits would earn you the proper credentials here. Unless you're made of money, we would have given you that degree..." she checked Lee's transcript. "Two years ago. And if I'm to be honest, I think you're overqualified."

Lee's heartbeat stuttered. He could not afford to blow this interview. "I think my broad study base is a perfect fit for Polytechnic Sixty-Two—"

The old professor cut him off. "Many of your studies were highly theoretical. We focus on practical knowledge here."

"And the salary," the HR woman piped in. "It might look good on paper. But even though you're a resident of the Benefit Sector, you'll need to pay income tax if you work here."

"Yes, of course," Lee said. "Otherwise Boomers would just roll in and take all the jobs." He spoke so candidly without thinking—scrambling to salvage yet another tanking interview—but it was when he acknowledged the politics of being a Boomer that the energy in the room shifted.

The Provost said, "When we hire, we're not just looking for someone to convey the subject matter. We want a professor who's an inspiration. A mentor. Someone willing to build a long-term relationship with students, beyond what you can achieve in a single semester.

"Listen," Lee said, "I know you think I'm just looking to round out my teaching credentials to land a better job in the Sector, but nothing could be farther from the truth. I'm at a major turning point in my life, a crossroads, and I'm tired of playing it safe. I want to be myself, I want to live my life, and teaching here is the best way to do it."

Too personal for a job interview, to be sure. The Provost and HR woman frowned, but the canny professor leaned in and said, "And what does your wife think of this career path?"

"I'm not married."

Understanding dawned on all three academics. The particulars? Maybe, maybe not. But it was plain that giving Lee a professorship was about so much more than a paycheck, and whatever the reason, he yearned for the intrinsic right for which the first Tax Rats had traded their benefits generations ago.

Freedom.

The professor said, "I think Mr. Kennedy's expertise would greatly expand our Language Arts department."

The Provost considered. "A provisional agreement on both sides, then. After the first semester, check in and see if we really are a good fit for each other. And if so, a long-term contract."

The HR woman shook her head. "I can't stress enough that once you take out taxes, the pay here is nothing like what you'd earn in the Benefit Sector. Many of our faculty get more value from the family tuition discount than their paycheck."

"Actually...." *People who don't haggle might come off like a sucker. No one respects a sucker.* "I require housing."

The interviewers exchanged glances.

"You have dorms—several buildings. I've seen them."

"You plan to live here," the Provost said, as if perhaps she'd misunderstood.

"Yes. I do. Forgive me if it's presumptuous to negotiate the terms of my compensation now—"

"If housing is part of the package," the HR woman said, "Then yes, we can certainly make you an offer in line with our other starting professors. But the dorms are old—nothing like the composite houses you're used to. And you would have to share a bathroom."

"But the room itself is private?"

"I can't vouch for its condition, but yes."

"Then if an offer is on the table, I'm definitely interested."

16

ON THE SHUTTLE HOME, Lee rehearsed telling his parents about his new job all the way back to the Sector. Once the professorship offer was made and accepted, he'd gone back to HR to fill out paperwork and look at the hard numbers. Income tax was just as steep as he'd been warned, so he'd negotiated discounted meals, three credit hours free tuition for himself, and an early move-in date two months before the start of the fall semester.

Polytechnic Sixty-Two seemed much more able to pay him in perks and bonuses—in *benefits*—than in cash. Lee suspected he'd actually appreciate those benefits now that he actually understood them for what they were.

He approached the only home he'd ever known. Already, the tidy row of composite houses looked small and sterile in comparison to the sprawling expanses of crumbling brick and wood on campus. In his mind, Lee had already moved to the Taxable District—yes, him, the man who was so sheltered he tried to pay for Orange Malt with a comb. The thought of living there was definitely terrifying. And yet, he had to admit...it was exciting, too.

Of course, there were a few more hurdles to consider. Moving his books and furniture. Stocking up on sugar.

Telling his parents.

The first thing Lee noticed when he walked through the front door was that the house smelled like soy sauce. That meant dinner would be stir-fry. Which meant Dad was cooking. Which meant Mom wasn't home...because she detested his father's attempts at stir-fry, even if she was too frugal to dump it down the compost chute.

Lee joined Dad in the kitchen, where ricey water was bubbling out from beneath a pan's lid. He turned the heat on that burner to low, and the lid stopped clattering.

"Had to make some last-minute recipe adjustments," Dad said. There was a recipe? "I keep forgetting Emma's gone."

And soon, Lee would be, too. "Did you have any plans together, you and Mom, for after we moved out?"

Most people would have taken the opportunity to ride Lee about the fact that he was still at home, but not Dad. He didn't have a sarcastic bone in his body. "You know your mother, she always had all kinds of plans. When we were young, she wanted to be an artist. Can you imagine? She even sold a little painting once—at your baby shower, in fact. One of her great aunts was admiring it and bought it right off the living room wall."

Lee had never imagined his mother's creative endeavors stretched beyond crafting. "Oh."

"We were just going to use your sister's old room for storage, but maybe Mom would like a studio instead. Somewhere other than the living room to paint and sew."

"Good idea." It was comforting to know that his parents would go on with their lives even after both he and Emma had moved on. "And what about you, any old hobbies you wanted to revisit?"

"Hobbies? I don't need to keep myself busy. I've got a family—that was all I ever wanted." Was it? Or was it just what he was expected to want? "When I went downtown to trigger the Algorithm and your mother's contact information came out of the slot, that tiny slip of paper was the first day of the rest of my life. We met the very next day. I remember your grandfather thought she was too old—she was almost thirty—but the Algorithm is never wrong.

"I'll never forget the first time I laid eyes on her. I thought, there she is, the mother of my future children, my lifelong companion, my soulmate. I'd been daydreaming about my Algorithm match since I was old enough to understand what weddings were about. And all that time, she'd been waiting for me, too."

Once you got Dad started, he did have a tendency to ramble. Lee sat quietly, listening to an extensive wedding anecdote he'd heard a dozen times before.

All the while, he was dying inside as a horrible realization crept up on him.

Yes, he could avoid marriage by fleeing to the Taxable District and accepting whatever tax penalties dodging the Algorithm would entail. But where would that leave his match?

He'd been so worried about himself, he'd never really pictured what would happen to the woman. Was she experiencing the same sorts of prejudices he was beginning to encounter? Housing, jobs...and that infernal question, when are you getting married?

Gosh, I don't know, whenever my gay Algorithm match

can't take it anymore, caves in to societal pressure and pulls the trigger.

Mom got home while Dad was in the midst of retelling the part about how he didn't know how to untie his tie, and she was too tipsy to help him. She sighed as if to say, *That old story again?*

Someday, Lee's Algorithm match would no doubt have a similar tale, one in which she had scarcely two months to plan a wedding because her husband had waited so long....

"What's with that weird look on your face?" Mom asked him.

"I got a job," he said hollowly, because he realized it no longer mattered. Hopefully, his match wouldn't be too traumatized about living in the District. "A full professorship."

Mom's expression was surprised. And then pleased. And then, in typical Mom fashion, brusquely pragmatic. "Well, I guess you'd better buckle down and finish writing that thesis."

17

THE WEDDING HALL WAS bursting with paper streamers and shiny balloons in burgundy and gold. Waitstaff circulated through the crowd carrying trays of champagne flutes. The waiters had Taxable District accents, the trays weren't silver and the champagne carried a sour aftertaste, but it was plentiful and cold, and that's what mattered.

Lee snagged another flute from a silvery plated tray, and downed it. His fifth glass? Maybe his sixth. It didn't matter. His response to "When are you getting married?" had felt foreign and ungainly, but only the first few times he'd said it. And now it flowed just as easily as cheap champagne.

One of his great uncles, a ruddy-faced man who used to bring lemon drops for him and gummies for Emma whenever he visited, wasted no time in getting to the subject everyone seemed so obsessed with. He leaned in and, over the drone of the band, said, "Congratulations, kid, after tonight, you'll be the only cousin not married. So get a move on, otherwise Mary's oldest is gonna beat you to it. Can't let yourself be lapped by the next generation."

"Don't worry. I've turned in my thesis, and I'm heading downtown to trigger the Algorithm tomorrow."

Behind Lee's head, champagne flutes clattered together as one of the waiters flinched. It was just a minor misstep—no cascade of champagne and broken glass with which to regale the kids when the wedding anecdotes were paraded out in moments of maudlin sentimentality. Only a tiny chime, like the tinkling of glassy bells.

Lee turned to find Roman staring at him over the tray of trembling flutes. His dark eyes were wide and his posture was rigid, making his shoulders look twice as angular. His lips were slightly parted...the only lips that Lee had ever kissed.

It was just a moment, the span of a single heartbeat, and then a barrier slid down behind Roman's eyes as he eased back into the role of the stranger. The servant. "Champagne, Sir?" he said, in an accent deliberately thick, with just the hint of a smirk.

Lee stared, guileless and blindsided. Eventually, Roman's cocky expression slipped. He turned away and lost himself in the milling crowd. "I don't pity you," Lee murmured. But by then Roman was long gone.

The ubiquitous band had been limping through an old standard, but it switched gears and launched into the preamble to the wedding march. Boomers, ever obedient, filed to their respective sides of the aisle to settle in for the ceremony.

When Lee approached his customary seat beside his sister, he was startled to find Howard there instead. He stood there staring as if he'd never seen the man before. The couple was holding hands, and their fingers were intertwined. It looked like a bear trap. Emma extricated her hand and told her husband, "Skootch down one and make room for Lee. I haven't seen him in ages."

Emma moved over, too. That would put Lee between his sister and mother—and he'd avoided sitting beside Mom at weddings ever since his own unmarried state became awkward. But now, he supposed, with his plan firmly in place, there was nothing left to do but fit himself in. Lee and Emma sized each other up for a moment, then at the same time, both blurted out, "Are you okay?"

Before either of them could react, the preamble wrapped up and the wedding march began.

His young cousin Beatrice rustled down the aisle in an absurdly poofy white gown trimmed in gold, hauling a massive bouquet of burgundy roses and gilded baby's breath. At her side, her Algorithm match, just as young, looked uncomfortable in his burgundy bow tie. Hopefully Bea wouldn't be too drunk to help him out of it later.

The vows and the documents were a blur. Lee attended a friend's or family member's wedding once or twice a month, ever since he could remember, and Bea's wedding was no different from any of the others. Maybe in Howard's social circles there was a budget for creativity and extravagance, but not here. Same band, same hall, probably the same chicken, too.

At least, Lee supposed, he knew what to expect on his own big night. Though the thought of kissing his Algorithm match—while Roman watched from the sidelines with a tray in his hand—made the sour champagne in his belly threaten to repeat.

At the Notary's command, the couple kissed. Awkwardly. But they came up smiling.

The music swelled and the newlywed couple bustled away for photos before planting themselves at the head table in the dining hall.

Dinner wasn't dry chicken after all, but rubbery beef with roasted potatoes. Maybe Beatrice was more of a rebel than Lee thought. Conversation at the table lit on him briefly as Mom regaled everyone with news of Lee's new job. They seemed confused when she proudly announced he'd be teaching at Polytechnic Sixty-Two. "Isn't that in the District?" one of his aunts wondered. But before the extended family could decide whether Lee had taken the job out of desperation or hubris, they were distracted by another round of sour champagne. Lee lifted his glass. The smell of acidic ferment made his throat flutter, so he excused himself and headed over to the bar for a proper drink.

He was wondering whether the vodka would taste like winter—like Roman's lips—when he realized the District bartender was looking at him a little too hard for polite scrutiny. And that he'd seen the curly-haired, broad-faced man before. "You're Roman's roommate," Lee said.

"Troy." He grinned. "And you're the guy who's so fond of toast."

So everybody knew how well Lee had fit the role of the insufferable Boomer. Fantastic. "I'm sure Spike was pleased to hear it."

"Yeah, she pretty much lives to be vindicated." Troy turned away to hand out a few beers, and by the time he came back, another familiar figure had slipped onto the barstool beside Lee: the Officiant Notary.

She seemed even shorter and stouter up-close, but that didn't make her any less intimidating. Although she was in his grandparents' generation, her hair was an unlikely shade of dark brown without even a hint of gray. She carried her weight like a weapon, and when she heaved herself up onto the barstool, even over the old standard the band was laboring through, Lee felt the furniture creak.

"Got anything to rinse the taste of that horrid champagne from my mouth?" she asked Troy.

With a faint smile—one that clearly wished it could be broader in polite company—he presented a bottle of Riesling for her inspection. She peered at it through her reading glasses. "Yep, that'll do."

Lee slid her a sideways glance. He'd always figured Notaries would be more, well...*formal*. He supposed he'd never actually encountered one who wasn't in the midst of officiating a ceremony.

Troy poured her a glass, filling it much higher than the customary third that wedding bartenders usually did, then tipped the bottle toward Lee.

"Have anything stronger?" Lee asked.

Troy waggled his eyebrows and produced a passable vodka from beneath the bar. In another life, Lee might have asked for sour mix, or ice. But with the acid champagne causing memories of Orange Malt to resurface, he had no compunctions about drinking it neat. Especially since that left so much more room in the glass for the alcohol.

"That's it," the Notary said, and raised her glass to Lee. "Drink up. It's a wise man who truly appreciates an open bar." She downed her wine and motioned for Troy to refill the glass.

Troy didn't mind her ordering him around. Instead, seemed genuinely amused. Smiling, he poured. "You must see a lot of weddings," he said.

"On a typical week? Five, minimum. In wedding season, sometimes more. Two a day, even three."

Lee wondered, briefly, if "wedding season" would

coincide with his Algorithm trigger. And then he decided it didn't much matter since it was all out of his hands, and knocked back his vodka.

Troy refilled his glass. He said, "I hear congratulations are in order today for a member of the bride's family, too. Mr. Kennedy here just finished his degree—after how many years?"

Lee realized the alcohol was hitting him when he tried to formulate a comeback and found he had no idea what to say. Not only had his family carefully crept around the implications—even Mom—but he was baffled that Roman and his friends took any interest in him at all.

Before he could fumble out some incoherent reply, the Officiant Notary declared, "I hope you like your chosen field, whatever it is. You'll be shoehorned into doing it the rest of your damn life."

"Kind of like marriage," Troy said, off-handedly.

The Notary nodded, staring into her wine. "The Algorithm matches you with your spouse, but whatever chooses the course of your life is even more cryptic and nebulous. Family. Tradition. Social station. All of that and more. Makes it feel like your whole existence has been plotted out, and the only thing left for you to do is force your way through the paces."

Lee fidgeted with his glass. Was the woman a Notary, or a mind-reader?

Troy topped off her Riesling. Again.

She downed a long swallow, then said, "It took me too damn long to figure out I wasn't responsible for other people's feelings. Let's say you come from a long line of bankers, and your whole family expects you to be a banker too. But you want to be a...a shuttle switcher. They'll just have to get over it, won't they?"

Lee supposed one of the positions in that equation correlated to "notary," but was unsure whether it was the "banker" or the "shuttle switcher." And he supposed if she'd wanted him to know, she would've come right out and said it. "But what if, theoretically, your happiness actually harms someone else?" he wondered.

"Well, obviously you can't get your kicks by going around and slapping people," she said.

Troy uncorked another bottle of wine and floated the question, "Let's say, theoretically, some Boomer decides he's not too keen on tying the knot. What then? It's not as if he's gonna hurt the Algorithm's feelings."

"It happens sometimes," the Notary said. "Nature versus nurture—when they meet, some couples despise each other even though they're genetically compatible. Lots of paperwork involved in getting an Algorithm re-trigger. Mountains of it. Not to mention the tax penalties."

Lee presumed he was drunker than he realized. She could not possibly have said what he thought he'd just heard. "You can re-trigger the Algorithm?"

"A do-over," Troy said. "I totally figured it was an urban legend."

Lee's heart started pounding. Hard. "And how could that even work? Does the Algorithm have to match each of them with another miserable couple somewhere, or...?"

The Notary turned in her barstool, wobbled, and righted herself. She looked Lee up and down. "Not at all. I thought you were an academic—didn't they teach you how the Algorithm works?" Maybe. But it probably sounded too much like math for him to understand. "You're thinking of a static system, like you're matched with a bride at birth and, voila! But that's impractical. People relocate. People die. And a few of 'em stay in school for a helluva long time. The Algorithm is dynamic. It takes into account all the best possible matches, *at the time*. So if your situation were to pull you out of the marriage pool, there's not some poor woman sitting around waiting for her ovaries to rot. Whoever she might have been, she's long since married off."

"Good to know." Troy slid Lee a meaningful look.

Lee clenched the bar to stop himself from leaping up off the barstool and letting out a victory cry. His Algorithm match, the poor faceless woman who'd been haunting him ever since he'd admitted to himself that he was gay, did not exist.

And that changed everything.

The Notary pointed to her half-full glass where it rested on the bar and said to Troy, "Don't touch that, kiddo, I'm not done." Then she toddled off in the direction of the bathroom.

The servers and guests who'd been swarming the small bar all night were suddenly absent too, and Lee was alone with Troy, who was still grinning. Had he known about the workings of the Algorithm all along? Hard to say what was taught in District schools...though he supposed he'd soon find out. "Why are you asking her about the Algorithm?" Lee demanded.

"Don't you find it all interesting? I think it's *extremely* interesting."

"You're mocking me."

"Me? Nah. I got nothing against Boomers. Sure, some of 'em are raging assholes, but you meet your fair share of assholes anywhere you go." Troy turned to fill a drink order while Lee examined his guilt. He must have been carrying it years, though he'd only realized it once he surrendered his first kiss to Roman in the kitchen. If he wasn't hurting anybody by leaving the Algorithm untriggered, he had nothing to be ashamed of—and the burden of that guilt and shame had been so ever-present, its sudden absence left Lee dramatically unbalanced.

The Notary heaved herself back onto her barstool, checked her wine, shrugged, and took a large swallow. When she set down the dwindling glass, Troy emptied the bottle into it and said, "So if there's a penalty for re-triggering the Algorithm, maybe it's best for *some people* to blow it off altogether. Y'know. People who just aren't the marrying type."

"That would be their decision," the Notary said.

Troy gave Lee a meaningful look. "But unless their pockets run deep—and I mean, *really* deep—what kind of life is that gonna be once they lose all their benefits? Not many Boomers can handle living in the Taxable District."

The Notary gave a pish-posh flap of her hand. "Rumor has it that one of the bride's relatives just took a position out at Polytechnic Sixty-Two. Most folks I know would have nightmares at the mere thought of driving through that neighborhood with their windows rolled up. So it's not common, no. But it can be done."

She checked her watch, finished her drink, and slid Troy a tip: a single dollar. Lee supposed he didn't have much use for cash anyway, though it was unlikely she had any water filters in her bag.

Without the Officiant Notary there to be a drunkenly oblivious buffer, Lee felt too exposed in Troy's knowing gaze, and he still couldn't tell if all that mirth being projected was at his expense. While he dug in his pockets for a shuttle token to leave and make his escape, in the gap left by the Notary, his cousin Jack elbowed up to the bar.

Jack was two years younger, but he looked older than Lee. Paunchy now, with a hint of jowls. Maybe reproducing at an alarming rate did that to a person. His wife was waddling around the dance floor, ready to drop their fourth child at any moment...hopefully not at the wedding itself.

Not many people had the patience or stamina to raise a double-sized brood in a small composite house. But Jack was playing the long game, and in twenty years or so, when the kids all moved out, he'd have accrued enough savings from their oversized-family benefits for early retirement.

Although he was still years away from realizing his goal, he seemed awfully smug about it. He sized up Lee with an air of superiority, and said, "So, Lee...when are you getting married?"

Maybe it was the alcohol. Drunkenness would be a convenient excuse for the answer Lee gave.

"I have a job waiting for me when the semester begins. My housing will be paid for, and I can even take classes from an entirely new curriculum. There is no wedding on the horizon, Jack. And you'd starve to death waiting to eat a piece of dry banquet chicken at any reception of mine."

As Lee slipped through the press of bodies and off to wait outside in the parking lot, he decided that, no, it wasn't really the vodka talking.

It was hope.

18

THE TWO MONTHS BETWEEN Bea's wedding and the start of the new academic semester were rough. Lee spent his time wrapping up his thesis. Funny how the motivation of needing the degree for his new job made the work he'd been dragging out for years come together in a few short weeks. The head of the department didn't read it after all, but Lee hadn't actually expected him to. The Masters in Language Arts was granted, and that's what mattered.

The dormitory where Lee had been placed was centuries old. But it was brick and concrete, rebar and steel, so it persevered. Its history had been painted upon the lobby walls, not in freeform District graffiti, but a calligraphic mural. Throughout its years on the planet, the building had been a dormitory, a troops garrison, a hospital and a motel. And now it was a dorm again.

As he hauled his last box up the stairs, a young woman with hair as pink as candy floss approached him. "Professor Kennedy? Hi! I'm Jasmine, the fourth floor RA."

"Happiness and hope, Jasmine."

She tittered—at his formality, or his accent?—but

seemed nice enough, regardless. "I'm here to help new students acclimate to dorm life, so make sure if there's anything you need, let me know. No curfew for you, obviously, but music or TV needs to go through your headphones after 10 pm. The room must be clear of food at all times to prevent the spread of vermin, but the dining hall is always open. The after-hours selection is nothing special, but you won't starve. This is the part where I'd go into a spiel about knocking points off your GPA if you're caught hoarding food.... Well, you can see the importance. Just don't do it."

Lee thought about the numerous vodka bottles stashed throughout his clothes. "What about alcohol?"

"No homebrew, but sealed carry-ins are fine. Just dispose of the empties in the proper recycling chute. Laundry facilities are in the basement, a communal study room on two, and this end of the hall is all faculty, so that'll cut down on some of the noise. Anyone who spends the night is your business—we're all adults here, and there's a condom dispenser in every bathroom— but divvying up your room and renting it out will get you in all kinds of trouble. Your room is huge—it was obviously a double—and it's easy money, but seriously, I wouldn't risk it. Any other questions?"

"Isn't the...ceiling...falling in?"

Together, they looked up at where the overhead plaster sagged, mottled brown and water-stained, and huge flakes of old paint hung in shreds. Jasmine didn't seem particularly alarmed. "Old construction, ya know. You can put in a maintenance request, but to be honest, they're so swamped, they're not gonna get to anything that isn't open to the elements. If it bothers you, feel free to fix it yourself."

With what? Lee almost asked, but then he realized

if he was going to thrive in the District, he'd need to stop thinking like a Boomer.

Collapsing ceiling aside, it was a better living space than Lee had hoped for. It was easily as large as his parents' living room, with two closets, two built-in desks, and plenty of space for a bed. Even a double bed.

For someone who'd been sheltered his whole life, Lee adapted to his situation readily. He was a quick study. Maybe switching his major so many times had done more than just hold off his matriculation—it had taught him to figure things out.

"Professor Kennedy?"

Lee opened his door to a young woman in leather pants, black lipstick, and a Weeping Bubo T-shirt. Oddly enough, she reminded him of Emma. "Happiness and hope. Please, call me Lee."

"Right. So, I'm Dot. Jasmine said you might want some help with your ceiling and...I'm *really* good with my hands."

"Great, come in and take a look."

It had been less than a week since Lee moved in, and already he'd assembled himself a bed from repurposed packing foam, and a shelf system from discarded crates. But the fabric he'd stapled over the worst parts of the ceiling had started to bulge.

"I've contained the crumbling plaster, but this solution is temporary at best. Do you have any ideas?"

Dot looked him up and down. "All kinds of ideas." She turned to the ceiling, assessed the bulge, then climbed up on the far desk, loosened the fabric's corner and peered beneath it. "Nothing's leaking anymore. Damage is really old. We'll cut out the disintegrating sheetrock and haul the debris, and those moving boxes in the corner will make a pretty solid patch."

People didn't decorate themselves with stickers, of course. Lee would have to ask. "Sounds like a lot of work. So how can I compensate you for your time?"

Dot slipped off the desk and dropped something onto the makeshift bed. A strip of condoms.

As if bartering wasn't confusing enough. Lee was supposed to offer something to her, and he didn't need condoms...and then he realized what she was in the market for. "Dot, you seem like really nice girl...."

"Not even a little—and that's the whole point. My roommate was banging this Sector guy, said he brought her off *four times* one night."

"That would take an incredible amount of lube and finesse." Before Lee finished the thought, Dot was yanking off her worn T-shirt, but he grabbed her by the arms and stopped her before she'd given him any more than a flash of brassiere. "Wait—I'd rather pay you in subway tokens."

"I can get subway tokens from the bursar."

"Dot, you're a student and I'm a teacher. You should be with your peers."

She jerked out of his grasp. "My *peers*?"

"Other students."

"I'm not *good enough* for you?"

"People your own age."

"Scared you'll contaminate your precious Boomer *dick* on some filthy *Tax Rat*?"

Dot swung around and made for the door, but Lee caught her by the arm and slipped in front of her, blocking her way. "Dot." He was hammering his plosives hard...and he didn't care. "Look at me."

She met his gaze with tears glittering in her eyes.

"First of all, I wouldn't have sex with someone within five minutes of meeting them, and you and I don't

know each other. But even if we did, I wouldn't do it."
At his words, a righteous indignation colored Dot's
cheeks, so he hastened to add, "I'm gay."

Dot's mouth dropped open. She stared him in the
eye for the span of a heartbeat, and then the fight
drained from her. She dropped her gaze to the scarred
linoleum floor and said, "I didn't know, Professor. I'm
really sorry." With that, she pushed past him, and fled.

Sorry about the contaminating his dick remark,
he supposed, and not trying to barter sex from him.
Which, if he thought about it a certain way, was somewhat flattering. He was mentally rehearsing what he
might say to put Dot at ease when they inevitably
passed each other in the hall or stairwell—or if he
looked out over his classroom and saw her chagrined
face looking back—when there was another knock on
his door. He presumed it was Dot again, calmed down
and reconsidering those subway tokens, so he was
surprised to open the door and find a stranger looking
back at him. A young man wearing lots of facial piercings, a worn leather jacket, and a knowing grin.

19

INFORMATION WAS, IN ITS own way, a precious commodity—but students shared it with one another freely. By the time class was in session, Lee suspected every gay man on campus had offered to fix the crumbling ceiling. And probably some who were merely curious, too. In the end, though, it was Dot who helped him patch the sagging plaster, and paint the repurposed boards a striking shade of chartreuse. A full bottle of Benefit Sector vodka earned not only her assistance, but her eternal devotion.

It was Dot who showed Lee how to bind the packing foam into a sort of mattress with some second-hand sheets and a box of safety pins. She then warned him that the makeshift mattress might begin to stink if it had no ventilation. She was also the one who showed him that six recycled plastic trays from the kitchens, the sort used for bread delivery, made a decent box spring if they were lashed together with duct tape. Together, they perched on the edge of his very bed-like bed and shared the final shots from his Sector vodka. He drank it straight up nowadays, and warm. And he definitely thought it tasted like winter.

Dot crammed her tongue into the shot glass to capture the last residue of clean, pure alcohol. Lee did the same. He was still working up the courage to visit Mom and Dad, and though he'd called Emma and begged her to visit, she'd seemed distracted and vague. Surprisingly, her avoidance hurt. Of the whole family, she seemed like the one most likely to venture into the Taxable District to see him.

Maybe it was just as well. Lee might be proud of what he'd accomplished in just a few short weeks...but he also remembered the way the District once looked to his privileged eyes, a patchwork of scrap covered in stickers and paint. While he saw his room as an accomplishment to be proud of, a Boomer might only see patched ceilings and bread pallets.

Dot kicked her heels against the floor, absently, staring off at nothing at all. "So, don't freak out or nothin'... but some guy's been poking around campus, asking about you."

"What guy? And what was he asking?"

"I dunno, some old guy."

"How old?"

"Thirty? Thirty-five?" She ignored the meaningful look Lee gave her. "Checking out rumors about a resident Boomer professor. But don't worry, we look out for our own. If he's casing your room, someone would notice, and he wouldn't get away with it."

"He's not looking to rob me."

"If you've got debts, we'll figure out how to settle them. With a family in the Sector, you've got access to all kinds of high-demand things. You know what? Maybe you should let me negotiate. I'll make sure he doesn't string you along and keep coming back for more."

"Thanks, Dot, but that's okay. I can handle this myself."

Lee set out after his last class of the day. The destination was a long walk from Polytechnic Sixty-Two, and normally he would have bartered for the use of a bike. But since he didn't know what he'd end up doing with it once he got where he was going, he walked.

The neighborhoods around campus were all familiar now. Dot had shown him how to scrounge things for his room. Pickings were slim, but she had a good eye. Tonight, though, he left a perfectly good bundle of shoelaces lying exactly where they were, and forged ahead.

His feet were sore and the sun was down by the time he got to Roman's building. Some of the neighbors' lights were on, but the windows in Roman's apartment were all dark. And so Lee propped himself against the security grate, and he waited.

The neighborhood was densely populated, and all around him, people came and went. He realized that although he knew better than to sit on the curb where he'd be an easy target for a mugger, he was no longer clutching his wallet and jumping at shadows. Roman's neighbors were just regular people with regular jobs. And if anyone was acting suspicious, it was Lee, lurking there against the building, waiting and watching.

He was nervous, worried that he might run into Spike first. Though now that he dealt with District students her age, he understood her posturing and bravado for what it was. Eventually, a figure rounded the side street and headed toward the building, all long legs and confident gait—easily recognized, even in silhouette. Lee's anxiety spiked, but he swallowed down his fear, pushed off the building, squared his shoulders, and stood tall.

Roman planted himself in front of Lee and gave him a long, appraising look. Lee realized he'd stood there for hours and somehow hadn't managed to figure out what to say, but maybe that was for the best. He'd never been much good at delivering a rehearsed speech without coming off as pedantic and stiff. Instead, he borrowed words from one of the most powerful nights of his life. "Someone told me a guy was looking for me… but my debts are settled and I'm not in the market for any batteries or pills."

"So it is true." Roman glanced at Lee's left hand, saw no wedding band there, then took a few steps back and really took him in. "You're a Tax Rat now."

Lee should have been offended at the slur, but all he felt was a sense of pride, and even a tenuous belonging. A few months ago, he would have scoffed at the notion of someone marking him by sight as a District resident, but now he knew it was entirely possible. He was no longer clean shaven, since space at communal sink was dear, and his brown overcoat was patched in blue plaid with yellow thread. "I'm still me," he said. "Just a man…trying to figure out where he fits in this world."

"Overthinking everything, as usual." Roman scuffed the sole of his boot against the sidewalk. "Formed any hypotheses yet?"

"I've got some ideas."

Lee reached for Roman and pulled him into a kiss. Roman stiffened, and Lee feared that maybe he'd read things wrong, and thinking that Roman still wanted him was nothing but hubris. But then Roman backed Lee against the security grate, grasped the old metal on either side of his head, and pressed their mouths together urgently. He kissed not just with lips and tongue, but his whole body. Eager and needy. Entirely sure.

Roman pulled out from the kiss and took Lee's face between his palms. His eyes glittered in the twilight and his hands smelled like rust. "Be with me."

"There's nothing I'd rather do. But not here." It wasn't the high narrow bunk, or even the likelihood of running into Spike that made Lee feel hesitant. It was the need to demonstrate, beyond the shadow of a doubt, that despite his upbringing, it was possible to change. And that not only had he allowed the change—he'd embraced it. "It's a long haul back to the dorm, but—"

Before Lee could even finish apologizing, Roman had spun away, stepped into the street and stuck out his thumb. A passing car pulled over. The window rolled down, and water filters changed hands. Roman cocked his head toward the backseat and said, "Well, what are you waiting for? Let's go."

No doubt the driver formed some opinion of the two of them exchanging nervous glances all the way to campus. Judging by the wolf-whistles and catcalls, the students came to certain conclusions as well. But Lee had earned another chance with Roman, and that was the only thing that mattered to him. It was like analyzing a single obscure word in a lengthy passage. Yes, the context was still there. But his entire focus narrowed to the one elusive concept, the single key to making everything else fall into place.

Lee unlocked the door and they rushed into his room. He'd hoped to give Roman the grand tour, but Roman was only interested in the bed...and not to admire Lee's scavenging abilities, either. Outerwear dropped to the floor, one scuffed leather jacket, one brown overcoat patched with blue plaid.

"Tell me what you want," Lee panted, as Roman raked needy hands up and down his back and ravished his throat. "Anything. I'll do it."

"Actually, I've been mulling over this scenario ever since I put two and two together, and realized the hot gay Boomer professor on everyone's flapping tongue was someone I already knew...intimately." Roman tipped Lee back onto the bed. Lee landed with a whoomph. The plastic bread pallets creaked, but held. "What I want is for you to lay there and do absolutely nothing."

Marital harmony was of the utmost importance, so the concept of capitulating to a partner's request—however strange—had been impressed upon Lee from a very young age. But he wasn't quite sure he understood what was being asked of him. "Is this some kind of roleplay? Am I pretending to be incapacitated? Are you going for a skewed power dynamic, or—?"

Roman clapped his hand over Lee's mouth. The tang of iron oxide tickled his nostrils. "No roleplay," Roman said softly. "You're you, and I'm me. And I'm gonna rock your world."

Being with Roman the first time, back in that cramped apartment, was indelibly branded into Lee's memory. And yet, he hadn't thought that there was so much more ground yet to cover. As Roman stood over the bed and peeled off his shirt, Lee realized he'd never properly seen the first person he'd ever kissed. The *only* person. Clothed, Roman was all hard angles and planes, but with the barriers stripped away, his physique was full of fascinating divots and swells where muscle played beneath the skin. He was wiry and hard, and the overhead light cast shadows that made each muscle stand out in stark relief. His skin was pale. And the flat expanse above his right hip bore a tattoo. A single word: Freedom.

He was stunning.

He didn't stand around waiting for Lee to admire his nakedness, though. As soon as he stripped himself down, he turned his attention to undressing Lee. Shirt, trousers, underwear, socks. None of it needed patching yet, not like the overcoat that snagged on a splintered railing outside the dining hall, but someday it would. And what a minuscule price it would be to pay for autonomy.

Roman rucked up Lee's shirt, but left his arms tangled in his sleeves. Lee squirmed as the trail of a hot tongue and the tickle of whiskers brushed across his chest. He half-recalled Ms. Carmichael's dull explanation of the common erogenous zones, but what he was doing with Roman here and now was so intense, it crowded out the memories of her benign voice. Where his education had been clinical, sterile, Roman was eager, even hungry. Lee shoved his shirt the rest of the way off and found Roman staring at him with cheeks flushed, and lips moist from tonguing his nipple. Disheveled. Erect.

"Stretch out," Roman told him. Lee reached for the edges of his mattress and felt his muscles lengthen deliciously. It had been such a long journey to come to this place, to finally be alone together in a space large enough to hold them both, it would've been a pity not to luxuriate in the moment.

"Can I speak?" Lee asked.

"I told you, it's not a roleplay. I'm trying to make a point."

"You've got nothing to prove."

"The hell I don't." Roman sank to his knees, half on the bed, and wet the head of Lee's cock with a hot swipe of his tongue.

Lee had been taught to give oral stimulation, but had never personally received any. He'd read about it. Seen video. Even imagined it himself during the lesson, in a vague and distant way, mostly to try to figure out what the point of it all might be. But nothing could have prepared him for Roman's mouth. The suction was dizzying and the delicious heat made him squirm, but pleasure was a fleeting thing. The unbridled intimacy of the act, however, would surely be scorched into Lee's memories until his dying day.

"Roman, wait," he gasped—just moments after they'd even begun—because his climax was coming far too soon.

Roman tweaked his nipple, pulsed it in time with the suction, and Lee arched up off the makeshift mattress and emptied himself in a startling, breathtaking peak.

Roman gentled his stimulation as Lee came...but he didn't exactly stop. Instead, he bided his time until the raw edge of sensitivity abated, and then he coaxed Lee to a state of eager readiness all over again. Lee had figured the story Dot told him about the Boomer who made his lover come four times had been embellished. Now, he wasn't so sure. Especially when Roman introduced the lube. His second climax felt just as urgent as the first, with Roman stroking his cock, fingering his prostate and sucking his balls. And the aftermath felt twice as heady. He sprawled there as if his insides were jelly, while Roman gazed down at him in evident self-satisfaction, and wiped the lube and semen from between his fingers on a hand towel that had once been part of a baby blanket, or maybe a bathrobe.

Roman rifled through his pockets and came up with another packet of lube. Lee somehow figured out how to form words again, and not just pleading sounds that urged Roman to go deeper. "You carry around an awful lot of lubrication."

"I could say I was hoping to get lucky, but in the right neighborhoods, this'll get you nearly as far as sugar." He trailed his fingertips down Lee's thigh. "And I'm willing to use every last drop of it making you turn yourself inside out."

Gooseflesh sprang up in the wake of Roman's touch. And then Lee's quiescent penis shifted, and began to swell.

The third orgasm was different from the first two, a much slower build with less direct stimulation. Roman flipped him onto his stomach with a pillow beneath his hips—the pillow he'd brought from his parents' home—and tongued his ass until his head spun, and he humped himself to completion. As Roman settled against his back, Lee gasped for breath, panting into the mattress. Sleep was beckoning now, or maybe it was just the dizziness brought on by hyperventilation. Either way, though, it was impossible to ignore the hardness now pressed along the cleft of his ass.

Roman traced his tongue across the back of Lee's shoulder, a lazy, meandering path, as if he was writing a secret message. Lee closed his eyes. His body hardly felt like his body anymore, but something foreign— detached, and at the same time, phenomenally present. "You're still hard," Lee murmured.

Roman gave a little grind. A kiss of preseminal fluid touched the base of Lee's spine. It cooled briefly before Roman's belly rubbed it away. "So, how much anal did they cover in those Boomer lessons of yours?"

"Just theory, really. Family planning."

"Which means...." Roman slid a finger between them and toyed at Lee's entrance. "This was uncharted territory?"

An exasperated laugh punctuated Lee's heavy breathing. "Believe me, you do not need to be jealous of my sex ed teacher. At all."

"Just figuring out what's what."

Sure.

Roman pressed his lips to Lee's ear and said, "I want to fuck you so bad I can taste it."

Badly was actually the word Roman wanted; given the fact that the bed was currently swimming in Lee's emissions, he highly doubted the experience would be anything but transcendent. But the correction fled from his mind as long, slick fingers began to stroke and tease. "First time can smart a little," Roman said, "but I'll take it slow—much as I want to pound you through the floor—and you'll see. It's worth it."

When Roman started bumping him in the prostate with each tender thrust, Lee had to agree. They labored together, clasped front to back—Roman struggling to make it last, Lee riding the knife edge of pleasure and pain. Their bodies moved in an intricate rhythm, some thrusts rocking in tandem, others syncopated and percussive, slick with sweat and stinging with pleasure, until finally Roman coaxed him to that precarious brink yet again, and then nudged him over. Roman filled Lee with his release, and Lee bucked into his hand until there was nothing left to spend.

They lay together, sated, numb, for a long moment. While Roman caught his breath, Lee began to drift, wondering how this vessel that had housed his mind all this time was capable of such exquisite pleasures, with him not even suspecting the extent of his body's boundaries. He turned his head, sluggishly, for a kiss. Roman's wet lips brushed his, sloppy, off-center, and Lee let his head fall back on the pillows.

"If you give me a few minutes to recover," Roman ventured, "I could go again."

If he'd been able to catch his breath, Lee would have laughed.

20

For someone who was accustomed to sleeping crammed in a closet with his knees slightly bent, Roman certainly took advantage of the opportunity to sprawl. Early morning was peaceful in the dorms. The distant sounds of students slamming doors and snoozing their alarms was pleasant background noise. The rising sun peeked through Lee's window, painting the far wall a warm pink.

"Tell me something," Roman said.

Lee hadn't realized he was awake. "Mm?"

"You knew where I lived. So how come you waited this long to see me?"

Lee watched dust motes dance in the sunbeam, then said, "I've always been sure about you. I was the one who needed figuring out. I didn't know if I could hack it in the District—maybe I was too privileged, too soft. And if it turned out I didn't fit in here—or anywhere—I didn't want to burden you with my problems."

Roman smoothed Lee's hair. "Guess we both had something to prove."

They lazed in one another's arms as long as they could, but Lee had a lecture in essay structure to deliver, and Roman was expected to report to the office where he filed papers three mornings a week. Even so, after a quick trip to the showers down the hall, a stray caress led to a kiss, which led to a fevered groping that very nearly caused both of them to be late. As Lee pulled on his work clothes—a button-up shirt and jacket, but no tie, not in the District—he said, "Next time, you're buying me breakfast."

Roman's eyebrows shot up. "I was kinda worried you wouldn't be so tasty once your squeaky-clean edges got roughened. Glad to see I was mistaken."

Lee was tempted to shove Roman back into bed and demonstrate just how edgy he could be...but a knock on the door interrupted them before the situation progressed beyond a kiss. No doubt the rumor mill had sent an intrepid student over for a first-hand look at the man who'd caused Professor Kennedy to fend off so many persistent advances. Lee was poised to tell whoever it was to mind their own business and get to class, so when he opened the door and found Emma on the other side, he was, for once, at a loss for words.

"I brought that vodka you were so insistent about," she said as she shouldered her way past him with a heavy tote bag in either hand. Behind her, Howard was lurking in the hall, looking clean, polished, and vaguely confused. Emma stopped three steps in and spotted Roman, sitting on the rumpled bed with his clothing slightly askew and his black hair sliding down over one eye. She opened her mouth. Shut it. Then turned to Lee and said, "Well, don't just stand there, introduce me."

Lee herded Howard through the door and shut it behind him, in case voices were raised. Not that they wouldn't carry through the walls to a certain extent, but it was common courtesy to play out family drama behind closed doors.

Since he first moved into the dorms, he'd been honest with his students. Everyone on campus knew he was gay. And yet, revealing this secret to his sister—someone he'd shared secrets with all his life—felt different. It felt bigger. Like telling Emma was as decisive a turning point as moving to the District. He would have preferred to do it in his own way, on his own time, rather than being forced into the revelation by her arrival on his doorstep. But when he looked at Roman, who had the twinkle of a smile brewing in his eyes, Lee decided he was just overthinking things again.

"Emma, Howard, this is Roman Sharp." He took a breath, steeled himself, and added, "I can't get married because I'm not meant to be with a woman, no matter what the Algorithm might say."

The meaning dawned on Howard in a visible slap. His eyes rounded and he gave a tiny gasp. Emma, however, didn't seem particularly surprised. She simply nodded. "And when were you planning on telling Mom?"

"I haven't really given it any thought."

"Uh-huh. Well, you can't just keep shutting her out of your life. Yes, this place might be decrepit, but it's perfectly safe, and you seem fine. I'll be sure to tell her so."

"Actually, it's really spacious," Howard said. Lee wasn't quite sure if Emma's husband was mocking him. Maybe not. Not only did the two of them seem comfortable together, but there was a guilelessness to his manner that was not unlike Dad's. "Look at the size of this window."

Emma went on. "Listen, Lee, you know Mom. She has to see for herself. And I think if you told her about

Roman, she'd understand why you're living here, and she could stop blaming herself for the way you turned out."

"I *like* the way he turned out," Roman said with a smirk. He was no longer the hired help, not on this side of the border, and he could say what he pleased.

Emma wasn't affronted—in fact, she agreed. She tousled Lee's hair and said, "We all do. But it's time to stop being so cryptic and weird with the family and tell them what's what."

Lee thought of his mother, bucking up and triggering the Algorithm (albeit at the last possible moment), moving in with a man with whom she had nothing in common, and cranking out the requisite boy and girl like every other obedient Boomer. "Mom would never understand."

"Don't be so sure." Emma set down a bag and pulled a cloth bundle from it. At first, Lee wondered why she'd wrapped the vodka so securely; it wasn't as if it was necessary to smuggle it in. But as she unrolled the corner to show him the blue and brown patchwork, he recognized it as Mom's latest quilt.

"Why are you giving this to me?"

"I'm not. Mom is." Emma shook it out, and he saw several borders had been added, enough to make the quilt far too big for a child's crib. She nudged Roman off the bed, heaved open the heavy quilt and shook it out. It flapped, then settled. It made the homemade mattress look substantial, even cozy. "When I told her I was having a girl first, she decided this one was meant to be yours all along."

It fit the broad bed perfectly. No longer a baby quilt—a wedding quilt. They looked at it together, brother and sister side by side, and Emma brushed her pinkie against his and added quietly, "She'll be glad to know you're not alone."

Lee watched Roman join Howard at the window and point out the various landmarks of interest that could be seen from their vantage point. Even in the soft morning light, he was all harsh angles and planes— dark, rangy, and vaguely dangerous. And Lee's heart leapt at the mere sight of him.

"*Not alone* doesn't begin to describe it," Lee murmured. "For the first time since I can remember, not only do I think of my future with hope instead of dread, but scarily enough, I'm actually...happy."

EPILOGUE

"WELL, IF IT ISN'T the Professor," Layla called out brightly.

Lee stood in the entryway of the Sugar Bowl Cafe and weighed the probability of someone who'd grown up in the Taxable District having seen a sugar bowl in anything other than a pre-Plague storybook. And then he conjectured how common it was in the District to keep bees. And then he wondered how beekeeping might be taxed—did the Office of Levee send someone out to count the insects? And all the while, his eyes raked up and down the hundreds upon hundreds of business cards tacked around the entryway.

Don't trust the ones that look bent up on purpose, Dot had advised. *The ones trying too hard to look old. Them are always scammers.*

Those, he'd said absently. And he'd counted himself lucky that his head had sustained no permanent damage.

It had been a relief to decide Layla hadn't set him up that fateful day. After a semester in the District, he'd begun to pick up on the nuances of the dialect's more subtle cadences. It was easier now to determine who was mocking him, and who was actually being pleasant. Layla had never been anything but sincere. Lee suspected she'd always seen his love affair with Roman as a modern-day Romeo and Juliet. Sans the poison...unless the Orange Malt were to be considered.

He found a seat where the glass baubles cast a spray of rainbows across the tabletop, brushed away a few ants, and turned over his coffee cup. Layla bustled over with the pot. "I see you been working hard on your stitching," she said. "You could get a pretty good side hustle going with that someday."

Lee ran a finger down his sleeve and traced the embroidery stitches his mother had shown him. Vines. Chains. Motifs. Blues, mostly. Some bright, some deep, some pale. All of them contrasted vividly with the dull brown of his overcoat. He'd started the embroidery at the cuffs. Soon the sleeves would be full, and he wouldn't need to feel so dowdy in the garment. By then, though, the summer heat would have set in, and he'd have no reason to wear it. He toyed with an embroidered paisley and smiled to himself, imagining the students' hoots and hollers when he rolled it out next fall, fully embellished. And then he considered how striking it would look with yellow accents, to match the stitching of the plaid patch. He'd have to see what shades of yellow were available on his next visit to the thread-pickers.

Before he was too far into his first coffee, Roman dragged out the seat across from him and fell into it, all angles and planes, one long leg sticking out precariously into the narrow aisle. "Thinking more of those deep thoughts of yours?"

Lee reached across the table and threaded his fingers through Roman's. "Maybe. Or maybe I'm just sitting here, enjoying my coffee and soaking in the ambiance."

Roman's sleek black hair slipped forward to hang over one eye. Lee's fingers itched to brush it back off his forehead, but he wouldn't be able to reach it without knocking over the condiment caddy. Besides, it would just slide right back where it wanted to go, anyway. "So, I've been thinking," Roman said...but then Layla came over to take his order, and chitchat about her brother's band, and make them both promise to be at the next Bonfire.

By the time they were alone again, Lee detected a bit of unease in the spaces between their words. With Roman, it was often helpful to pay attention to what he didn't say. But Lee was in no hurry. He simply nursed his watery coffee until Roman was ready to speak.

"So...one of the old geezers back at the office is retiring, and this knucklehead from the mailroom got promoted to take his place."

Lee nodded and sipped his coffee.

"The mailroom," Roman muttered.

Layla brought their plates. Lee ate lightly at the diner since his meals were included at the dorms, but the Sugar Bowl's pie crust was a lot flakier than he could get on campus, where everything was slopped together in bulk and the students either didn't know, or didn't care. By the time he'd captured the last crumbs of pastry on the back of his fork, Roman was ready to say what was really on his mind.

"That job would've been mine, if I had my MBA."

And now Lee saw the real issue. There was an obvious solution—he'd often noticed Roman was tacitly intrigued by his lesson planning—but Roman had needed to come to the decision on his own. Lee gave his coffee an extra squirt of sweetener syrup and stirred, acting as if his interest was merely casual.

In a rush, as if he'd possibly rehearsed it a time or two, Roman said, "The thing is, I can fit my jobs around the program if I juggle 'em, but there's no way I can afford both rent and tuition."

Lee nodded.

"And so I was thinking—look, stop me if I'm out of line—if I enrolled, Polytechnic Sixty-Two wouldn't stop me from moving in. With you."

Funny, how Lee had cataloged such a great variety of *tells* Roman gave when he was nervous. The tightening of his jaw. The jiggle of his knee. The way his eye contact didn't quite click. Then again, maybe it was no surprise these things weren't apparent at first glance. There were so many things Lee had been blind to.

"We'll keep a ledger," Roman hastened to add. "I'll pay you back."

"And have a reputation as a money-grubbing Boomer come back to haunt me by charging rent to the man I love? My students would never let me live it down." Their eyes met. Roman wanted to protest, Lee could tell. "Although, you're not entirely off the hook. I fully expect you to pick up the tab for lunch."

Roman smiled, a fleeting thing he tried to quell, though sometimes Lee did manage to get a glimpse. "You drive a hard bargain, Professor Kennedy."

"I do my best." After all, haggling was expected, and Lee was keen to adopt the local sayings and customs. He'd spent far too many years shielding himself from the Algorithm and avoiding what might be. Now that he could truly immerse himself in the experience— now that he was free to finally live—he could embrace his life, as it truly was, in all its colorful imperfection.

ABOUT THIS STORY

OFTEN, WHEN I GET stuck in my writing, or a scene just feels flat, I'll retire to paper and pen, and journal about "five different ways this scene could be different," or some other riveting theme like that. But what I do to give myself a little spark of inspiration is open a dictionary, stick my finger inside, and pick a random word for each point. Sometimes the words I land on are so silly, it makes it very hard to write a potential scenario around it. But that's okay. The whole idea is to get myself thinking in a new, and hopefully more interesting, direction.

There are also plenty of apps and websites out there that will generate random words, photos, names, and other useable bits that can be cemented into the mosaic of the story. I find the finger-in-book method works best for me at the moment. But tomorrow I might fall in love with a randomizer app. The specific source doesn't matter, as long as it gets the ideas flowing.

Imperfect Match started as a palate-cleanser of a short story I intended to crank out between two larger novels. It was inspired by the random word prompt *utopia* and *elope*. In the original short, I had Lee meet

Roman and elope *away from the utopia* on his sister's wedding day. But then I sat on the story for a while, because it seemed like this tiny glimpse of Lee in that moment—the one in which he realized why he'd been dragging his feet in regard to the Algorithm—was pretty pivotal, but I wanted to explore more of his world.

Now, I can't imagine the story without all the colorful settings from the District: the bookshop, the Bonfires, the cafe and Polytechnic Sixty-Two.

Random fact: I named the university after a public grammar school near my grandmother's house, School 62. I thought nothing of it when I was a kid, but looking back now? A bunch of numbers—what a drab and utilitarian way for a city to name its schools! I see on Wikipedia that School 62 closed in 1980, and nearly all of the Buffalo numbered schools are defunct now. Times change.

There's something about Lee Kennedy I find really endearing. I suppose it's the fact that he was willing to do whatever it took to be true to himself, no matter how daunting the learning curve might be. It was an absolute joy to arrive at the point where he earned his students' respect, and blossomed into a man who finally had something other than a tax write-off and a sperm donation to offer a potential partner.

ABOUT THE AUTHOR

Jordan Castillo Price is more likely to show up at a bonfire than a wedding, though she is easily swayed by cake.

Visit jordancastilloprice.com to see what else she's got up her sleeve.

MORE STORIES BY JORDAN